DARKE ACADEMY
BLOOD TIES

GABRIELLA POOLE

Hodder
Children's
Books

A division of Hachette Children's Books

A Catalogue record for this book is available from the British Library

ISBN 978 0 340 98925 8

Typeset in Berkeley by Avon DataSet Ltd,
Bidford on Avon, Warwickshire

Printed in the UK by CPI Bookmarque, Croydon, CR0 4TD

The paper and board used in this paperback by Hodder Children's Books
are natural recyclable products made from wood grown in
sustainable forests. The manufacturing processes conform to the
environmental regulations of the country of origin.

Hodder Children's Books
a division of Hachette Children's Books
338 Euston Road, London NW1 3BH
An Hachette UK company
www.hachette.co.uk

The Darke Academy series:

1 Secret Lives

2 Blood Ties

and coming soon . . .
3 Divided Souls

PROLOGUE

'Hey, kiddo. Are we keeping you up?'

The voice sounded familiar, but somehow muffled and distant. As if it was coming from the bottom of a well. With an effort, Cassie Bell forced her eyes open and blinked woozily at the sight before her. The table was set with thirteen places. At the centre sat a pasty-looking turkey, clearly only big enough for eight. Cheap supermarket own-brand crackers and a paper tablecloth. Fatty chipolatas and overdone sprouts.

Christmas, Cranlake Crescent-style.

Could it really be only three weeks since she was eating exquisite French cuisine from fine china and crystal in the elegant dining room of the Darke Academy? It seemed a lifetime away.

'What's the matter?'

Cassie refocused on the sandy-haired figure across the

table. Oh, yeah. Patrick. Her key worker. The only thing that had made coming back to her old care home bearable. She managed a smile.

'Aren't you hungry, Cassie?' piped up Jilly Beaton sweetly from the head of the table. 'That's not like you. You've been eating us out of house and home for a fortnight.'

Cassie dug her nails into her palms. Jilly's bitchy remarks had been increasing ever since she had got back from Paris. Normally, Cassie wouldn't have given her the satisfaction, but her fuse seemed to be getting shorter every day.

'Yeah, well I just lost my appetite,' she snapped, pushing her chair back and getting to her feet. 'Excuse me.'

'Cassie Bell, you're not excused—' began Jilly, but Cassie was already out of the room.

Patrick caught her at the foot of the stairs, his face full of concern. 'Cassie, what's up?' he said. 'You've been acting funny ever since you got back from Paris.'

Cassie paused for a moment. Where would she even begin? Tell him the truth about the Academy? About the mysterious group of students called the Few and their dark secret? About the ancient sprits that shared their bodies, instilling power and beauty but demanding in return that they draw life-force from their ordinary, human roommates? Could she tell him about what had happened to *her* in that black place beneath the Arc de Triomphe – the interrupted ritual that had left part of the spirit that had lived in the body of Estelle Azzedine lodged in her own mind? Could she tell him about the strange, driving hunger that had been growing inside her ever since, and how she knew that turkey and chipolatas just weren't going to hit the spot . . . ?

Impossible.

'I'm just missing my friends,' she mumbled. 'Y'know?'

An expression of relief washed over Patrick's face. 'Of course you are. Have you spoken to anyone today?'

'I had an email from Isabella last night. And one from, um, Ranjit.'

'Who's Ranjit?'

'Just, uh, a boy in one of my classes,' replied Cassie, flustered. 'Why?'

Patrick's grin grew wider and his blue eyes glittered. 'Because you blushed when you said his name.'

'Oh, give over!' Cassie gave him a playful shove.

'He's not your boyfriend, then?'

'No, he's not,' she said hurriedly.

'Uh-*huh*.'

'No. Really.' Cassie twisted her fingers into the

cashmere sweater that her friend Isabella had sent her for Christmas. 'It's . . . complicated.'

Ha! That was the understatement of the century. Her few snatched moments with Ranjit at the end of term had hardly given them time to define their relationship. All she knew was that her stomach twisted with longing every time he came into her mind, but that he was back home in India. Thousands of miles away. She'd just have to put up with missing him – missing him like she could die of it. The feeling was so strong Cassie almost surprised herself.

Absorbed in her memories, she jumped at the sound of her ringtone. Pulling her phone from her jeans pocket, Cassie almost dropped it when she saw the name on the display. She felt the blood rushing to her face again.

'Speak of the devil . . .' chuckled Patrick as he slipped back into the dining room.

Cassie winced inwardly at his choice of words. She still didn't understand what the Few truly were. What Ranjit truly was. *Gods and monsters*, he had once joked bitterly. So which was he? Cassie didn't know. She wasn't sure that he knew himself.

Pushing her worries out of her mind, she clasped the phone to her ear like a lifeline. 'Ranjit!'

He must be able to hear the stupid grin she was wearing, even half a world away.

'Cassandra.' The soft warmth of his voice made her forget the freezing sleet and even, for a moment, the raging hunger. 'Happy Christmas.'

'Same to you.' Breathless, she sat down on the stairs. It was criminal how much she missed him. Criminal, and deeply inconvenient. 'Oh, it's good to hear from you.'

'Are you OK?' He sounded concerned.

'I'm fine. Fine. Just a bit . . .'

'The hunger is growing, isn't it?'

Cassie was quiet for a moment. It was a relief to speak to someone who knew what she was going through. Ranjit had been there before.

'Yes,' she said at last, and laughed shakily. 'You got it.'

'It won't be long, Cassandra. A week and a half. Will you be all right?'

'I'm fine. Honestly. I just . . .' She hesitated, then took a leap of faith. 'I miss you. A lot.'

'God, me too.' The vehemence in his voice was shocking, coming from the normally cool and collected Ranjit Singh. He almost sounded relieved. 'I miss you and I'm *worried* about you. Have you, ah, heard any more from Estelle?'

Cassie swallowed. Ranjit was the only person who

knew that the ancient spirit sometimes spoke to Cassie inside her head – something unheard of among the Few. 'Once or twice. But the old bat's been quiet lately. I hope she's curled up and died of hunger.'

'I don't think that's going to happen, Cassie.'

'Yeah. I know.'

'Take care of yourself. Please?'

She smiled, couldn't help it. 'Course I will. And I'll see you soon.'

'Can't be soon enough.' He gave a low laugh. 'Listen, I have to go. I'll talk to you again when I can.'

Tears stung her eyes as her stomach twisted again. 'Bye, Ranjit. Merry Christmas.'

'And you. Again.'

Cassie snapped the phone shut before she started to blub. She buried her face in her hands. Oh, this was ridiculous. She was supposed to be *tough*. She'd get through this. The hunger to feed, the hunger for Ranjit . . .

Stop. *Stop*.

The trouble was, she was ravenous. Overcome with a desperate, intangible hunger for something beyond mere food. But there was nothing she could do except wait it out until the new term began. Then she might get some answers. And perhaps the waiting might help. Hell, if you stayed off chocolate long enough, you lost the craving for it. If you lasted a few weeks without cigarettes, you didn't want them any more.

Yes, and if you give up breathing for a while, you'll lose the taste for oxygen!

Cassie stiffened.

Well, really, my dear. You do amuse me!

Ignore her, Cassie told herself. Ignore her.

Easier said than done. Just the sound of Estelle's voice in her head was enough to send the hunger sweeping through her with renewed force, so that she almost lost her balance, tipping forward.

She heard a door open and close. Footsteps. A voice . . .

'Cassie? Are you OK?' Patrick's tone was concerned.

She leaped to her feet, fists clenched. *OK?* Why did he keep asking her that? Of course she was *OK*! His constant flapping around her was really beginning to grate. He should stay out of it, if he knew what's good for him.

No! What made her even think that? Patrick was only trying to be thoughtful; he had done so much for her.

Estelle's whisper was like the caress of a serpent. *And he could do so much more, my dear.*

Patrick looked nervous under Cassie's steady, feverish stare. Yes. Estelle was right. A good friend like Patrick would always give of himself. She could rely on Patrick. He was strong, young, confident. Full of life. Perfect.

'Cassie?'

She was just so damn *hungry*. Her lips stretched into a rictus smile. 'I'm fine.'

Don't talk. Let him come closer. I can smell him . . .

Patrick took a pace back, and she thought she saw him shiver. 'Stop messing about, Cassie. Your dinner's getting cold.'

You seem warm enough to me.

'OK, I'm sorry. I'll leave you in peace.' He was turning away. 'Come back when you're ready.'

'*STOP!*'

She launched herself from the step, almost flew after him. Seizing his collar, she yanked him back, spinning him around. Her fingers found his jaw, gripping him, tugging him towards her. He tried to pull away, but he didn't stand a chance. Not a chance. Since the ritual, she was stronger than she'd ever been. More than strong enough to overpower this . . . mortal. Cassie laughed out loud.

Patrick's eyes were full of terror, and his panicked breath was in her face. She could smell him again: oh, the *life* of him! Her lips were pulled back when she caught sight of a figure beyond the glass panel of the front door.

8

For an instant, her heart seemed to stop, and she stiffened and growled a challenge. A face snarled back at her, feral and mad, like a rabid animal. And then, with a sickening jolt to her gut, she knew. It wasn't some monster trying to break into the house. It was her own reflection.

'Oh my God!' She let go of Patrick so fast he crumpled to the floor. She stumbled back and away from him.

His terrified eyes were locked on her, the bright blue dilated almost to black. She expected that. But she didn't expect the words that fell from his mouth.

'Oh God, Cassie. Not you. Not you!'

What?

For half a second she stood, hands over her mouth, staring at Patrick. Then she turned on her heel and fled. She didn't slow down as she took the stairs two at a time, crashed into her room, furiously grabbed a chair and jammed it under the handle. There. That was as safe as it got. As *he* got.

Cassie slumped to the floor, exhausted. It could have been worse, she told herself, as her heartbeat slowed. So much worse.

Who was she trying to kid? She'd lost control. She could have hurt Patrick. Killed him even. Jamming her fists into her mouth, Cassie bit down until she drew blood. A few more days, that was all. A few days and she'd be back at the Academy. Back with its mysterious principal, Sir Alric Darke. He must be able to help her fight this. She'd see no one until then . . .

But Cassandra, my sweet, I must FEED!

The plaintive, angry voice echoed and bounced around her skull, which felt so light and empty. She was dizzy with hunger. But she'd control it. It was just a few days. Only a matter of time . . .

That's right! In the echo-chamber of her head, Estelle sounded vindictive and starved, but triumphant. *Oh yes, Cassandra, my dearest girl! Only a matter of time . . .*

CHAPTER ONE

The carousel jolted into life as baggage spilled on to it. Cassie stood penned in the crush, overwhelmed with the sheer noise and bustle of JFK, desperate to spot her tatty suitcase so she could get the hell out of there. A tall, sweating businessman on one side, a mouthy old lady on the other, both of them shoving and manoeuvring, hanging like vultures over the turning baggage belt. Neither seemed like prime candidates to feed upon, but beggars couldn't be choosers . . .

Oh, no. Stop that! Cassie wanted to cry but she didn't have the energy. Tucked tightly into her window seat, avoiding looking at the passenger next to her, she'd seen the dawn come up behind the Statue of Liberty as the plane had circled in, but she hadn't cared. Hadn't cared about the symbolism of it – sunrise on her own New World. Hadn't cared about the beautiful symmetry and skyline of the city. She'd just wanted the plane to land so she could draw a clean breath of air, a breath that hadn't been round everyone's lungs already so that it *tasted* of them. She'd just wanted to be gone from that crush of humanity, crammed into the aircraft like an untidy life-force buffet.

Well, at least she'd controlled her appetites. Seven hours. That was something to be proud of, wasn't it? That was an achievement.

Of course, my dear! And you were so right. I'm glad we restrained ourselves. Airline food. So dry and tasteless.

Cassie spluttered a tight laugh out loud despite herself.

'Hey, honey, wanna move along there?' The businessman barged her out of the way to seize his case.

If she hadn't staggered sideways into the resentful old lady, she'd have fallen over. Now she could feel herself swaying, her reserves of strength almost gone. The man's stale perspiration was overwhelming. The sour-and-salty tang made her nostrils dilate. It was only sweat but it was infused with the vitality of him. He was hot and his overburdened heart was pounding: she could hear it, *feel* it. Oozing out of his pores, his scent clung to her nostrils like . . . a plate of chips. Yes, that good. Cassie licked the upturned corners of her lips, focused on his, watched his breath pant out and in . . .

Cursing, he pushed past her, banging his case on her shins, and was gone. Missed her chance. Tears sprang to her eyes, and Cassie didn't know if they were tears of relief or fury.

Missed! No! We missed him! Estelle sounded half-demented. *Find someone. Find someone NOW!*

Vaguely, Cassie was aware that her own case had just swept by, held together with a recognisable old bungee of Patrick's, but she took no notice. She was scanning the crowds hungrily now, and she wasn't worrying about anything any more. Anything except—

That one! That one, quick!

Turning dizzily on her heel, she locked on to the figure Estelle meant. It was young, strong, female. Slender but toned, and striking in a dark Mediterranean way. It had a child with it but the child was passed into its father's arms with a kiss and a word and a smile, and now the young, strong female was turning with a *click-click-click* of heels and making for the toilets.

Not *it*, she! yelled Cassie inwardly. *She!* She's a human being—

Yes, yes. Whatever. She! Quick! WE'LL MISS HER!

Backing up swiftly, hunger jarring against the thrill of the chase zinging through her veins, Cassie pushed her way through the crowd and followed the *click-click-click*.

Funny that she could hear it so acutely through the noise and the bustle and the endless distorted public announcements. It was as if her whole being was focused on the sound of those heels, every nerve in her body locked on to the female. A little way ahead, it – *she* – swung open the door of the toilets. *Click-click-click.* Cassie quickened her step, silent in beaten-down trainers. Almost there. Almost there!

HURRY!

Yes, Estelle, we'll feed. We'll FEED!

'Cassie!'

The shriek of greeting penetrated her concentration. Just. Her purposeful steps wavered.

'Cassie Bell! *Darleeng!*'

A mosquito. Buzzing, bugging. She wanted to swat it, kill it. Leave me alone, she wanted to scream. I need to—

Something barrelled into Cassie, knocking her off-balance and enveloping her in a warm, expensively scented hug. 'CASSIEEEE!'

For a fraction of a second Cassie fought the embrace, throwing a starving glance at the toilet door as it clunked gently shut on the human and its life-force.

Then she came back to herself with a jolt that was almost painful. What had she done? What had she nearly done!

'Isabella?' Close to tears, Cassie returned her tight embrace, hanging on to her best friend as if she was all that was keeping her sane.

Yes, this one, then! She'll do! She'll do, I tell you!

NO! Her inner snarl was fierce enough to shut Estelle up. For now.

'Oh, Isabella. Am I glad to see you.'

'And I you! Did you come off the London flight? It landed five minutes before the one from Buenos Aires! Serendipity! Wonderful!' The girl was still talking in constant exclamation marks, thought Cassie fondly as Isabella tossed her glossy mane of silky brown hair. 'And Jake is waiting for us! I have texted him, he is outside, in the terminal!'

'And you stopped to say hello to me?' Cassie raised her eyebrows weakly. 'I'm flattered you didn't run over me to get to him.'

Isabella had doted on the handsome New Yorker ever since he'd joined the Academy. Having finally got together at the end of last term, the pair had barely had a week together before Isabella flew home to Argentina (first class, natch). If she was impatient to get her hands on Jake now, it was hardly surprising.

'Oh, Cassie!' Isabella laughed, but her eyes darkened a little as she held Cassie's shoulders and studied her face. 'You look so beautiful. Too thin, yes? But very, very beautiful.'

'Gee, thanks. Flattery'll get you everywhere.' She grinned weakly. Her head was really swimming now. It was the excitement, she told herself. And the jet lag. Whatever. She just needed to be calm for a while.

But Isabella was laughing again, still bubbling over with enthusiasm. 'I can hardly wait for us all to be together again! You and me and Jake! Yes? Come on, let's go!' Abruptly she released Cassie.

'Sure. Let's . . . go . . .'

But that was easier said than done without Isabella's supporting arm. Swaying, Cassie felt her knees buckling under her. She'd have hit the ground if Isabella hadn't caught her elbow in her strong polo-player's grip.

'Cassie? *Cassie?*'

Cassie frowned. Isabella's voice seemed to have gone all funny over Christmas. Weird. Distant.

Fading.

Or maybe that was herself. In the dark now. In a cold, black void.

And disappearing . . .

CHAPTER TWO

'Cassandra? Cassandra!'

Another familiar voice. She couldn't place it, but it was powerful, reassuring. She'd be all right now, she knew. Maybe because she was dead. She must be dead, because the airport hubbub had vanished and she was floating in a serene bubble of calm.

'Cassandra!' The gravelly tone was more insistent now. A hand slapped her cheek, then the other one. 'Cassandra, come back.'

Against her will, she forced her eyelids open, groaning. The blurred face was just as familiar as the voice. Ascetic, fiercely handsome, and frowning with concern.

'S'r Alric . . .'

'That's right. Wake up.'

Blinking against bright light, Cassie levered herself up, clutching cushions for support. A sofa. A huge leather one. For a moment she thought she really was dead, and in an especially comfortable afterlife, because she could see nothing but acres of blue sky. Then she registered the glass walls surrounding her, and skyscrapers glittering in the morning sun, and the wintry treetops of . . .

Central Park!

Above the trees the sky was diamond blue, streaked with white wisps of plane trails. She blinked woozily at her very own angle on the spectacular New York skyline.

Or rather, Sir Alric Darke's angle.

She came to properly, with a jolt. Tried to stand up, but fell back. She heard a little yelp of relief, and Isabella was at her side again, flopping down next to her and hugging her. Cassie gazed blankly around at the plush, stylish office.

'What a *fright* you gave me! Oh, Cassie!'

At last her companions were coming into focus. Isabella, of course – and Jake, standing close by, looking hugely relieved if a little wary of his surroundings. As she met his warm brown eyes, he gave her a weak grin. 'Hey, Cassie. Good to see you.'

'Jake. It's good to see you too.'

That wasn't strictly true. Cassie was *more* than just glad to see him – she was overwhelmingly relieved. Last term, Jake had discovered more of the Few's secrets than it was safe for any outsider to know. Cassie hadn't been sure if he'd ever come back to the Academy after finding out that his fellow pupil and the former object of his affections, Katerina Svensson, had murdered his sister, Jessica. The temptation to blow the whistle on the institution that had covered up the crime and let the Few girl off with mere expulsion must have been overwhelming. Yet here he was, standing in the principal's office.

What had brought him back? His affection for Isabella? A strange sense of transferred sibling loyalty to Cassie, the girl who everybody said had looked *just* like his dead sister? Or was he back to deal with the 'unfinished business' he'd spoken about at the end of last term?

Her feeble smile for Jake faded as she turned, a little reluctantly, to Sir Alric. He hadn't changed – his handsome features as striking as ever. There was something strained about his grey eyes, and he didn't smile, but he didn't look angry either.

'Hang on – how did . . . ?' Cassie rubbed her forehead furiously. The last thing she remembered was the baggage belt grinding by, the smell of human sweat, the crush and the heat. And *needing* something. Needing it so badly she'd abandoned . . .

'My case! I left it! I didn't—'

'It's OK.' Isabella flapped a dismissive hand. 'I picked it up for you.'

'But how did you—'

'It's the right one, don't worry.' Isabella giggled. 'I knew which one was yours. I'd recognise that slaughtered old thing anywhere.'

Cassie shook her head, perplexed only for a moment. 'Knackered, Isabella. My *knackered* old case. But security? Immigration? How did you—'

'When you fainted, Isabella contacted me straight away,' explained Sir Alric. 'I have connections in the Department of Homeland Security who were able to expedite matters.' He shot a guarded glance at Jake, as if he was afraid to say too much. 'Now, I'm sure you wish to be with your friends, but first we have issues to attend to, you and I. Isabella and Jake, please. I must talk with Cassandra. Alone.'

Isabella and Jake glanced at each other doubtfully. Cassie tried to look up to give them both a reassuring nod, but the mere sight of her two friends was enough to bring the hunger shooting back through her like a lance, taking her breath away with its ferocity. Staggering to her feet, she stumbled against Sir Alric. His hand fell on her shoulder in what might have seemed like a kind gesture of support – except that his fingers were gripping so tightly he was bruising her. Cassie barely noticed the pain though; she could feel the tautness of her own muscles, coiled like springs in her desperation to feed, and she knew Sir Alric was actually restraining her.

'Now, Isabella, Jake. Please leave us.'

Jake frowned at the steely edge of the principal's tone. 'I'm not sure . . .' he began.

'It's OK, guys.' Cassie reached out and took Isabella's hands, squeezing them a little too hard. 'I'll be fine. See you soon. Promise.'

'You're sure?' asked Jake, eying Sir Alric with open hostility.

'Sure.' In fact, she wanted them gone, desperately. She wasn't sure how much longer she could last without pouncing on one of them. 'Honestly, Jake. Please go, it's fine.'

Taking a breath, the young American took Isabella's hand. 'We'll be outside. See you *soon*, Cassie.'

'Yep,' she said weakly, gritting her teeth into a smile. Oh please, please GO!

She had a last glimpse of Isabella's worried face as the door shut behind her friends, and then she closed her eyes, swaying with hunger.

Cassie felt Sir Alric's hand pressing her back on to the sofa, and she managed to prise open her eyelids in time to see the sinister and ugly porter Marat coming towards her, bearing a small leather case. Where had he appeared from so silently? She propped herself groggily forward.

'You need to feed, Cassandra.' Sir Alric's voice seemed to echo around the room as Marat gently set the case down on the mahogany coffee table in front of her.

'I can't.'

'You've gone weeks without it. You're dying. I should never have let you leave at the end of last term, but I didn't expect this. I don't understand why the hunger in you has grown so fast, but it has. And you *must* satisfy it.'

Too weak to cry, she put her face in her hands, moaning. 'I can't.'

'You must,' snapped Sir Alric fiercely. 'You think you're being selfless; in fact you're being self-indulgent. I'm sorry for what happened to you, Cassandra. I'm sorry you were tricked into this. But I have a responsibility to the Few spirit as well as to you.' He nodded to Marat, who slipped a silver key into the front of the case.

Unsteadily, Cassie followed the porter's movements. The lid of the case bore a symbol that she recognised immediately: a two-inch pattern of intricate, interlocking lines that she'd seen before, branded on the skin of certain select students at the Darke Academy – as well as blurred and broken on her own shoulder blade. She didn't know what the pattern meant, but she knew what it denoted.

It was the mark of the Few.

Marat lifted the lid and Sir Alric stepped up to the case, gazing reverently at the row of crystal phials inside. Each one was also engraved with the Few mark, and was beautiful enough on its own – but the translucent contents glowed like liquid pearl, sending shimmers of light through the delicate crystal. For a moment Cassie was so mesmerised that she almost forgot her ravening hunger.

Sir Alric nodded to the porter again. The small container Marat drew from his pocket couldn't have been more different from the lovely case: a white plastic clip-lid box. Snapping on latex gloves, he flipped it open without ceremony and withdrew a sealed plastic packet. This he tore open, producing a disposable syringe.

Cassie's eyes widened. 'What's that?'

Sir Alric too was donning gloves, and he had turned cool and businesslike. 'Call it an interim measure, Cassandra.'

Delicately, Sir Alric inserted the needle into one of the phials and drew out a small measure of the pearly liquid. 'You must learn to feed. But this,' he said, lifting the syringe, 'will give us a few days' respite.'

'What is it?' She eyed the needle with dread. 'What is that? I won't let you put that in me!'

As she tried to squirm aside, Cassie felt powerful hands grip her shoulders, pressing her back against the sofa and holding her in place. Marat. He'd moved behind her and she couldn't get away. God, he was strong, his vice-like hold too strong to escape, but she still struggled violently as Sir Alric approached her. For an instant she saw regret and sympathy in his face, then it hardened.

'Be still. This is the only way. It's for your own good, Cassandra.' Sir Alric's voice was entirely cold as he leaned over her wriggling, kicking form. 'And for everyone else's, too.'

She felt his thumb rub a spot on her arm, then the hot sting of the needle.

Cassie feared for a moment that she'd been electrocuted. This must be what it felt like, mustn't it? A savage current running through her, bringing her so fiercely alive she couldn't think clearly. Coldness raced through her veins, followed swiftly by heat – and strength. Shrugging off Marat's hands, she sprang up, her body rigid, her fists clenched. The awful, tearing hunger had vanished, as if she'd been released from constraining jaws, but her vision had turned to a blinding blur, spots dancing in front of her eyes as she lost her balance and again collapsed on to the leather upholstery, squeezing her eyes shut to try to clear her vision . . .

When she opened them again, Sir Alric sat in an armchair, facing her, his fingers steepled under his chin. Marat and the case had gone.

'So, Cassandra. How do you feel?'

The memory exploded into her mind. She sat up angrily. 'What was that stuff? Tell me what it was!'

He didn't react to her fury. 'It's a distilled solution. From the tears of the first Few, a thousand and more years ago. Do you think I offer it to everyone? Consider yourself lucky. It's extremely powerful.'

Cassie took a breath, absorbing the news. Not drugs, then. Not poison. Maybe something that could help her . . .

'So I can do this instead? Inject that stuff instead of feeding from other people?' Her eyes lit as relief swept through her.

'No,' Sir Alric said abruptly. 'This is a one-off. What you saw in the case is all that exists. There is no question of you having it all. You will learn to feed. Like the rest of us.'

The despair returned in double measure, her brief new hopes crushed.

Taking advantage of her stunned silence, Sir Alric

stood up. 'You cannot starve the spirit that is inside you, Cassandra. Without the Tears, you would soon have reached a crisis point. When the desire to feed finally got too much, you would have lost control and attacked someone. That person could have been hurt, or even killed. And it could have been anyone.' He paused for chilling effect. 'Including Isabella and Jake.'

'I didn't know,' she gasped. 'I didn't realise.'

'Of course not,' replied Sir Alric, his voice softening slightly. 'That is what the Academy is for, Cassandra. It is my duty to teach each new member of the Few how to feed safely, so they are no danger to themselves or those around them. When the time comes, I will do the same with you. But for now, the injection has given you some breathing space. I think you needed that. So I'll ask again: how do you feel?'

'Better,' Cassie admitted. 'Much better. Can I go now?'

'Of course. Your friends will be worried about you.'

'They're just outside. They said they'd wait.'

Sir Alric smiled wryly. 'I'm afraid you've been asleep for most of the morning, Cassandra. Your friends left more than two hours ago. I explained to them that you needed to rest, although Mr Johnson took quite some persuading. They'll be down in their rooms now, I imagine. You have a great deal to discuss with them.' He paused. 'Especially Miss Caruso.'

'What do you mean?' said Cassie, her voice tightening.

'Cassandra, your stamina astonishes me. You fought the hunger for far longer than I could have expected. But now your luxury of choice is at an end. Except, perhaps, in one respect.'

'Oh?' Cassie raised her head.

'To learn how to feed safely, you will need a partner – a life-source, if you will. That is why all students who are members of the Few are assigned a roommate who is is not. So you have a decision to make, Cassandra. You may move in with a new roommate, one to whom you have less . . . emotional attachment.' Sir Alric lifted his hands in an elegant shrug. 'Or—'

'Don't say it,' she blurted.

'I must, Cassandra, I'm sorry. You must learn to feed on Isabella.'

CHAPTER THREE

The atrium was spectacular. It couldn't be more different from the Academy in Paris, but this Upper East Side building had its own breathtaking architectural beauty, all sleek glass and marble. The building's height was dizzying, seeming to turn and sway as Cassie stared up to the glass roof high above her. The sky beyond was still such a gleaming blue it made her feel faintly giddy. The clean, modern lines of the walls were softened only by the pool and foliage in the centre of the atrium.

Cassie grinned, pausing to dip her fingers into the cool water and stare up at the figure in the middle of the fountain. 'Hello, old girl,' she whispered to the bronze sculpture. 'Haven't got rid of that bloody swan yet, have we?'

Leda, of course, didn't react, still reaching dreamily for the savage god-swan above her. At her bronze feet, water trickled out of the stone. Ferns and trailing plants grew in a wild profusion, twining round rocks and spilling on to the polished marble. And among them, of course, were the orchids. Cassie touched one black petal with a fingertip. Sir Alric's little pets, Ranjit had called them. That figured. Sir Alric liked the beautiful, the rare, the dark . . .

Cassie was surprised how pleased she was to see all the other familiar statues. In the winter light that flooded in from Fifth Avenue, they gleamed alabaster white from their places around the edge of the vast central hall: Achilles and Hector; Narcissus; Diana and Actaeon. And the one that always chilled her spine: Cassandra and Clytaemnestra. Cassandra, the girl who nobody believed. Cassandra, who entered a house that smelled of blood . . .

With a shudder, Cassie remembered huddling beneath that statue, waiting to feel the bite of Keiko's knife. Yet here she was now: in many ways the same as the homicidal girl who had helped Katerina murder Jake's sister. Now she too was a freak – maybe even a monster, like Keiko. She wasn't feeble Cassandra any more, the helpless little victim. She was closer to the bloodthirsty Clytaemnestra. One of the Few.

And what did that mean, to be one of the Few? Cassie gazed at her reflection in the water. Back at the airport, Isabella had suggested that she had grown more beautiful. Cassie hadn't noticed any change, but now she looked closely, perhaps her cheekbones were slightly more defined, her yellow-green eyes more striking.

But she knew that there was more to the Few than just pretty faces. She had seen their superhuman strength and fighting skills at first hand. And now that the constant hunger to feed wasn't drowning out all other sensations, she could feel some of that strength in her own muscles, making her feel relaxed and confident in a way she hadn't before.

Beauty, strength and confidence – a heady combination. But all dependent on the feeding. Draining the life-force from some innocent person.

Sucked dry . . . That was what Isabella had said when she'd told Cassie about Jessica's death. Her body was *damaged*. Was there a chance Cassie could do that to Isabella in turn? No. She wouldn't – couldn't – let that happen. But Sir Alric had made it clear that Cassie had to learn to feed.

So she couldn't go on being Isabella's roommate.

But she couldn't bear that. Isabella was her best friend.

So she'd have to learn to feed safely from Isabella.

But if something went wrong . . .

It was impossible: Cassie's mind could only lead her in inescapable loops. Around her, other students were hurrying in for the new term, gossiping and bitching and laughing, trailing chauffeurs and expensive luggage in their wake. Could she share a room with one of those spoilt brats? No – it was unthinkable, and no doubt they'd say the same. Frustrated, Cassie turned to go. Colliding with a warm body, she was caught and held.

'Oh! I'm sorry.'

'Don't apologise.' The voice was warm, familiar, amused – and it sent her heart into orbit.

'Ranjit!'

Before another word could pass her lips, Cassie found that they were suddenly pressed urgently to the handsome boy's own. Her eyes closed, and she could feel Ranjit's hands pressing into the small of her back, his mouth moving against hers. She felt herself rising on to the tips of her toes, her fingers tangled into his glossy black hair, pulling him towards her, and she could hear Ranjit draw breath sharply through his nostrils as he kissed her more and more deeply, wrapping his arms tightly around her.

It was only when they lost their balance and stumbled into a gawping first year that Cassie felt Ranjit's arms loosen. Blushing fiercely, Cassie released her own grip and backed out of the embrace. For a moment she was unable to speak, let alone meet Ranjit's eye – though she could feel the incredulous gaze of the students surrounding them. And she could certainly hear the barely stifled whispers that erupted around the atrium.

'I'm not believing what I'm seeing . . .'

'Oh. My. God.'

'Him? Him and *her*?'

'Ranjit Singh? I knew he had a thing for scholarship girls, but I mean . . .'

Ranjit cleared his throat, and Cassie finally looked up at his sheepishly grinning face.

'I guess that cat's well and truly out of the bag, then,' he chuckled.

Tentatively, he reached out and put one hand on Cassie's shoulder, steering her off to a corner out of the collective stare. Cassie hadn't imagined her heart could beat any faster than it already was, but it leaped again at his gentle touch.

'Yeah, looks like it,' she replied. 'Sorry . . . I'm not sure what happened there.'

'Um, neither am I.' His golden-brown skin flushed. 'I missed you,' he laughed. 'If that wasn't obvious.'

Cassie couldn't repress a huge smile. 'Me too. It was a long Christmas, eh?'

'You're telling me.'

She wondered if he was mocking her a little, but his

face was as sternly beautiful as always. There was something else in his expression too, a yearning that matched her own. Damn, he was hot. A voice on a mobile phone was one thing, but she'd forgotten the sheer animal presence of him. She could practically sense his heart beating faster, and she knew instinctively that he wanted to touch her again – almost as much as she wanted him to . . .

Whoah, Cassie!

Without even thinking about it, she'd stepped towards Ranjit and caught herself just before she could fall into his arms again. This was going too fast. After what had happened, she was a little embarrassed. Maybe even a little scared.

Estelle's promise came back to her. *You'll never have to be scared of anything again, Cassandra . . .*

Not strictly true. She'd managed to scare herself, getting carried away like that in public. She felt herself flushing as she imagined the eyes of the whole school on her.

'Cassandra?' Ranjit looked a little wary himself. Like her, he'd taken half a step forward before he stopped himself.

'Sorry,' she mumbled. 'Guess absence made my heart grow even fonder than I'd thought.'

Ranjit laughed. 'I know what you mean!'

'Look, maybe I should go and, um, freshen up. I haven't found my room yet, and I should say hi to Isabella properly. But we could meet for a coffee later?' she ventured.

'Yeah. That's probably a good idea. Five o'clock?'

'That'd be great.' She checked her watch. 'Actually, how about four-thirty?'

He grinned. 'Four-thirty it is!'

'Great. See you then.' As she smiled and turned to walk away, Ranjit reached out suddenly and took her hand gently in his. The warmth of his skin sent a fresh flutter through her body.

'Wait. Before you go – you're OK, right? At Christmas when we spoke on the phone you sounded . . .'

'I know. I'm fine now. Honestly. I'll fill you in this afternoon.'

He held her gaze for a moment, as if to make sure she was telling the truth. For a moment there was a suggestion of the roiling, fiery glow she'd seen in his eyes more than once, but Cassie couldn't look away. His hand squeezed her fingers more tightly. The gurgling trickle of the fountain seemed amplified, and the sound of expensive heels on marble. Then the shrieking giggle of a Year Nine made both of them jump. Releasing her hand,

Ranjit shook his head self-consciously and smiled.

'If you say so.'

'I do. I'll see you later for that coffee. I'm buying!'

'OK. Where are we going?'

'Don't sound so nervous, rich boy.' She winked. 'This is New York, isn't it? I'm sure I'll find a suitably *seedy* joint.'

Ranjit's deep, honey-tinged laugh echoed around the atrium. God, she thought, you could bottle that sound and sell it to lonely girls the world over.

'Find me a seedy joint then, Cassandra Bell. I'll meet you back here.'

'Don't be late.' She gave him a mock scowl.

He grinned. 'I wouldn't dare.'

Well, she'd done her best to introduce Ranjit to the sleazy and the downbeat, but they didn't seem to be part of *this* New York. Sir Alric certainly had his standards, and he'd obviously brought the Academy to this neighbourhood for a reason.

Out on the streets, staring up at the gigantic buildings in wonder, with her breath pluming in the frosty air, Cassie happily let Ranjit take over the hunt. Coffee, after all, had only been an excuse to be alone with him; that, and to experience the city she'd missed on her arrival. She could forget for a while about monsters and demons.

Walking north on Fifth Avenue, just one anonymous couple among the brisk and smartly dressed crowds, she could barely choose where to look next – so it was just as well Ranjit seemed to know his way around. He steered her down East 78th Street to Madison Avenue and a chic and glossy café that served a bewildering selection of coffees to chic and glossy customers.

'Jeez. You're paying after all, I'm afraid.' Unwinding her scarf, Cassie raised her eyebrows at the price list as they ordered.

'It'll be worth it.' He nudged a mug towards her. 'Though why you'd want to put cinnamon syrup in fine coffee, I can't imagine.'

'Mm-mm. Good as the Tears of the Few,' she murmured mischievously, relaxing a little for the first time. 'Perks a girl up no end.'

Ranjit blinked in surprise. 'Sir Alric gave you the Tears?'

'Oh yeah.' She winked. 'I'm a special case, me.'

'Wow.' Ranjit shook his head anxiously. 'Did he mention—'

'That I can't do it all the time? Yeah, he did. Thanks for the reminder.' Cassie's jaw clenched. So much for feeling relaxed.

'So now you've got to learn to feed.'

'So I'm told.'

'Right . . . um . . .' Ranjit seemed to read the displeasure on Cassie's face, and played for time by swallowing hot coffee too quickly. Sucking in a breath, he winced. 'Is it going to be Isabella?'

'I don't know. Look, do we have to talk about this now?'

Ranjit smiled apologetically. 'No. Sorry.'

Cassie took a sip of coffee. She didn't want to be angry. Not now, not with him. With a sigh, she set down her cup and ran her finger round the rim of it. 'How much time do you reckon I've got before I have to decide?'

'A few weeks. Maybe less.' Ranjit lowered his voice to a murmur as a waiter passed by. 'Your hunger has developed faster than anyone could have predicted. It's incredible, Cassandra.' With something like admiration, he added, 'Unprecedented!'

'You sound like Sir Alric,' Cassie replied. 'And not in a good way. He's the only other person who calls me Cassandra. Well, apart from . . .'

'Estelle,' Ranjit finished. 'Would you rather I called you Cassie?'

'You know what? I think I would.'

'Then I will. Cassie.' With a smile, he put his hand over hers.

Damn, she thought. That did feel good. And strong. And supportive. Slowly she linked her fingers into his.

'You never wanted me in the Few, did you?'

'No, I didn't. I didn't want you involved in any of this.' He smiled ruefully. 'But it's done now.'

'And I would have been involved anyway,' said Cassie, with sudden realisation. 'One way or another. It was Isabella who was supposed to be initiated, wasn't it? She was the obvious candidate. So I guess I would have been *her* life-source?'

Ranjit's hand tensed. Then he nodded slowly, his eyes roaming her face. 'Perhaps. But I would have done what I could to stop that too.'

Cassie frowned. She'd have preferred that scenario to the one in which she now found herself. Wouldn't she? If Isabella *had* joined the Few – if she'd asked Cassie to be her life-source – what would Cassie have done?

She knew perfectly well what she'd have done. She'd have refused. Run a mile. Screamed the place down and called the cops.

As if reading her thoughts, Ranjit said, 'You know, you can feed without her knowledge. Even though she knows what happened to you, there are ways round—'

'No,' she said firmly. 'I'm not going to lie to my best friend. Sir Alric says he'll teach us both.' In a mutter she

38

added, 'If she agrees, I mean . . .'

'It's for the best, Cassie. You have to know how to feed safely. And if it's done right, it really doesn't do any harm.'

Shutting her eyes, Cassie gave a frustrated moan; then she felt Ranjit's hand squeeze hers once again. He sighed deeply and turned to Cassie with an attempt at a smile.

'Look, I'm just glad you're here, and you're OK. We'll get through it . . . together.' He leaned over and kissed her gently on the lips, lingering for a moment before pulling away. 'And about *this* . . .' he murmured, pressing his forehead to Cassie's.

'Yeah?' Her voice was hoarse.

'I think it might be a good idea for us to try and take it slow. I mean, I don't know what happened in the atrium but it felt almost . . . out of control?' He looked cautiously at Cassie, and she nodded and smiled.

'It did. Not that I'm complaining.'

'Me neither. It's just that, given our circumstances and . . . past experiences, I just don't want anything to go wrong for us. We should be careful.'

Ranjit ran a reassuring hand along Cassie's arm and turned to drain the rest of his coffee. Cassie stared down at her own barely touched drink. She'd hardly thought about it before, but the way he'd said *past experiences*, and the expression on his face when she mentioned that she had been destined to be Isabella's life-source, spoke volumes. How could she have forgotten?

Jessica.

Jake's sister had been involved with Ranjit before she died. In fact, she was meant to be meeting him the night she was lured to her death. The girl who finished up drained of her very essence by Katerina and Keiko was the same girl everyone said looked like Cassie. The thought of it made her head spin. OK, this could be weird.

'Cassie?' Ranjit's voice brought her out of her reverie. 'We should get going. You look tired.'

His beautiful face smiling down at her, and his hand gently laid on her shoulder, made her head spin once more – but for the right reasons.

This is ridiculous, she thought. You're not Jessica. It's not the same. Don't talk yourself out of this before it's begun.

Forcing a smile, she stood up. 'Tired? Come on then, I'll race you back to the Academy!'

CHAPTER FOUR

The corridor was dark. Cassie was running, urgently searching for something. Someone. She rounded the corner into yet more darkness. No, not darkness – two eyes, glowing red, were there ahead of her. Looming out of the black. Coming towards her. No. She was moving towards them . . .

There he is, Cassandra! Grab him. Take him, He's the one for us. Don't let him convince you otherwise. We belong together. We need him.

Cassie's arms reached out blindly, snatching at the void.

You don't want to be alone, do you, Cassandra? Reach for him. Grab him. We don't want to be alone. We want them both. You and I, he and his . . .

'Ranjit?'

Cassie's voice was a growl, echoing through the empty space. She lunged forward once more, her hands grabbing on to something. Shoulders: hunched, muscular. His bare skin almost burning under her touch. Then his arms, encircling her, squeezing her until she could barely breathe. Her fingernails like claws, digging into the flesh of his back.

Yes, Cassandra. Don't let him go! We mustn't let go!

'I won't.'

You won't. You won't? But you've abandoned me! Why have you abandoned me, Cassie? There's a part of me alone, you know. The part we left behind.

'What? I'm here! Estelle?'

You felt that void, didn't you, dear? Only for a little time, but you felt it. Imagine being trapped there. It's not nice. Why are you being so unkind? Poor, poor Estelle. Are you going to let me stay out here, Cassandra? Are you going to keep me apart? Keep us apart?

HOW COULD YOU?!

Cassie woke with a start, shaking. Throwing off the blankets, sweating and gasping for breath, she sat up straight and raked her fingers through her hair. It was still dark: the faint glow from outside was street lighting.

It was a nightmare, that was all. Cassie sighed. With all that had happened, it was a wonder she hadn't had more bad dreams. She gave a wry half-smile. Sometimes it seemed like her whole life now was a bad dream. It didn't help that she had Estelle inside her head, messing with her mind. Although all was quiet now, so maybe the spirit had spent her fury for the time being and Cassie could sleep in peace.

Still, her heart continued to thrash, and it wasn't just from fear. She had a terrible sense of sadness, guilt and regret in the pit of her stomach, almost in spite of herself.

Poor, poor Estelle . . .

Cassie rubbed her fingertips against her temples, groaning inwardly but not making a sound in case she woke Isabella. Part of her *was* sorry for Estelle. When the ritual that was supposed to bind them together forever was interrupted, part of the Few spirit had been left stranded outside Cassie's body, divided from the rest. Ever since, Estelle's voice had begged Cassie to let her in. But even if she knew how to do that, Cassie was far from certain that she wanted to. Fractured visions of the Few woman's past revealed her to be proud and strong, yes, but also vindictive, cruel and selfish. If she joined fully with Estelle, how could Cassie be sure that she wouldn't follow the same path?

Fumbling for the tumbler of water on her nightstand, the back of Cassie's hand bumped against one of her framed photographs. Irritably, she picked it up to move it aside, and froze.

43

Something was wrong. The frame felt strange beneath her fingertips. She brought it close to her face. Even in the dim glow of an artificial dawn, her hand trembled.

The metal frame had melted. That was how it looked, anyway. Twisted, buckled and warped – as if it had been left too close to a fire. The grinning faces of Patrick and the Cranlake kids had melted into hideous masks. Alarmed, she reached out to touch the nightstand. It was quite cool. Cassie swallowed hard. Swinging her legs down on to the floor, she picked up the other photograph, the one she had surreptitiously taken of Ranjit at the end of last term. It too was badly distorted: the silver frame looked as if it had turned liquid in the night then re-solidified, like candle wax. And Ranjit's shyly smiling face – it was unrecognisable.

She stroked it remorsefully, tears springing to her eyes. What had she done?

Hang on. What made her think *she'd* done anything?

A feeling, that was all . . .

Miserably, she cursed, but not far enough under her breath. In the other bed Isabella stirred and stretched, yawning. Cassie had barely enough time to shove the melted pictures under her pillow before Isabella blinked sleepily. Her roommate yawned and smiled.

'Morning, Cassie. Mmm . . .' Abruptly she sat up.

'Hey! We're in New York!'

Cassie shook her head. She instantly felt a little more cheery. How could Isabella be bursting with such enthusiasm at this hour? Her friend hadn't changed since Paris – which was kind of nice, when so much else had. Affecting a drawl she said, 'Chill, honey. It's six o'clock in the morning. Ain't sun-up for an hour.'

Isabella rolled her eyes. 'Cassie, that accent is more South Carolina than South Bronx and even I know it. Now . . .' Slumping back on to her bed, she rubbed her hands with glee. 'What shall we do today?'

'Um, apart from start school, you mean?' asked Cassie.

'Yes, yes, apart from that. This is the City that Never Sleeps! And neither should we!'

'Uh-huh.' Cassie didn't bother mentioning she already had a head start in that department. 'You know the first class is maths, right?'

'No. No, no, no! I shall not even think about it!' wailed Isabella. She paused and then gave Cassie a sidelong glance. 'We need to talk about you, Cassie.'

'Oh, God.' Cassie sighed. 'Not again. First Ranjit, now you as well. Can't we talk about someone else?'

Isabella folded her arms crossly. 'Cassie. I let you off yesterday because you were meeting your Indian prince – which you need to fill me in on as well, by the way.' She paused to give Cassie a wink. 'But I know you're not telling me something. You fainted at the airport! You did not look so terrible and starved just from missing breakfast or having a bug. It's because of what they did to you, isn't it? At the Few ceremony?'

Cassie rubbed her neck. 'Yes,' she mumbled.

Isabella nodded, her eyes narrowing. 'Right. And what have you done about it?'

'Sir Alric had a . . . er . . . solution.' Cassie smiled brightly, hoping an explanation would stall Isabella's questions for now, even if she was being economical with the truth. She needed time. More time. 'Literally, I mean. A liquid solution.'

'You mean drugs?' Isabella's hand flew to her mouth. 'Cassie, I'm not sure—'

'Please, Isabella, it's nothing to worry about.'

'Oh?' Isabella folded her arms and raised an eyebrow. 'If it is nothing to worry about, why are you still so unhappy? I know you better! Why are you so nervous and sifty?'

'Shifty . . .'

'Out with it, Cassie Bell!'

Defeated, Cassie went over and slumped on to Isabella's bed. 'Remember what I told you about Keiko and Alice last term? About seeing Keiko kind of feeding

46

on Alice? Well, that's how the Few stay alive.' She sighed miserably, trying to avoid meeting Isabella's eye. 'They draw life-energy from someone who's non-Few. And, apparently, that's something I'm going to have to do too . . .' Cassie trailed off. She hadn't the heart to carry on any further, to ask the question out loud.

Isabella didn't reply. Maybe, thought Cassie, she was remembering Cassie's horrible description of Keiko draining the life out of her helpless roommate. Or her boyfriend's sister being *sucked dry* . . .

The air seemed to crackle with tension as the silence stretched on and on, but Cassie couldn't bear to look up to see the horror and revulsion on Isabella's face. Any minute now, it would all be over. Isabella would leave the room. She'd go to Sir Alric and demand a change of roommate. Of course, she'd say they'd still be friends, but she'd never quite forget what Cassie had asked of her. She'd never quite forgive—

'OK.'

'What?' Cassie wasn't sure she'd heard correctly.

'I said OK. You will feed from me.' Seeing Cassie's incredulous expression, Isabella flapped her hands. 'Look, I'm not saying this is ideal. One thing is for sure, I had a *very* different view of the Few before I knew all this craziness was involved. But another thing I know for certain is that you're not like Keiko. Not a *bit* like her. She was insane. You, on the other hand,' Isabella grinned, 'well, you have your moments. But you are my very good friend, Cassie Bell. If this is what you need, then this is what *we* need to do.'

Cassie could only stare at her. 'Isab—'

Isabella interrupted, holding up her hand. 'Hold on. Alice did not know what Keiko was doing, did she?'

'No.' Cassie picked at a chewed nail. 'The Few have a special drink. It makes your roommate forget everything. They think it's kinder.'

Cassie finally made herself look at Isabella's face, but there was no disgust on it. She was nodding, intent and serious.

'Yet you don't want to deceive me, Cassie. You have told me everything, and that shows you trust me. Thank you. So I will be honest with you, because I trust *you* too.' Isabella raised a warning finger. 'You must never give me this drink. I won't ever be tricked or lied to.'

'Isabella, I don't know—'

'Cassie, you need to feed. That's obvious. It's why Sir Alric is so worried about you, yes?' Isabella grasped Cassie's hands.

'He – yes. He said he'd teach me, show us how to do it safely.'

'Well, Sir Alric is a good man. He knows what is necessary and what is or isn't dangerous. Don't worry, Cassie.' Isabella's smile was cautious but sincere. 'If he shows us how to do it right, then it will be fine. I'll be your . . . what do you say?'

Cassie swallowed. 'My life-source. But wait, Isabella. What about Jake? He'll never allow you to do it.'

'Jake is not my boss, he's my boyfriend,' sniffed Isabella. 'You're right, he won't like it, but this is my decision. I am not Jessica and you are not Keiko. And anyway, maybe what he doesn't know won't hurt him.'

'You can't keep it secret from him, Isabella.'

'Why not? A girl is entitled to some secrets,' Isabella replied, her dark eyes flashing. 'When the time is right, I will tell him. He will understand.'

Cassie stared at her roommate. Wasn't this the perfect outcome? She'd been honest with Isabella, and Isabella had agreed freely.

So why did she still feel like a piece of dirt?

'All right.' Cassie breathed out and smiled. 'Thank you. Thank you, Isabella.'

'You're welcome. Just make sure you don't overindulge.' Isabella grinned. 'I am sure that my life-energy must be very strong stuff!'

'There's no way in hell I'm getting anywhere *near* you

until Sir Alric's taught me everything there is to know about this feeding thing.' Embarrassed, Cassie bit her lip self-consciously. How had they come to this?

Isabella looked at her roommate and giggled.

'Your face is a picture, Cassie Bell. It will be *fine*. Besides, being one of the Few is not all bad news, huh? What about Ranjit? I heard how he swept you off your feet in the atrium yesterday. Surely he is *some* comfort?' She grinned wickedly, and Cassie couldn't help but smile too.

'Look,' Isabella continued, her eyes sparkling with mischief, 'I wish this whole Few thing had not happened. But it *has* happened, and you're *in*. And seeing as it's Fate Accomplished, you might as well have some fun being Few, no?'

Cassie was about to correct her when she thought: no, Fate Accomplished is quite appropriate.

'Isabella, I'm not going to start throwing my weight around.'

Isabella sniffed. 'Hmph! Since Christmas there isn't enough of you to throw.'

Cassie smiled wryly.

'And of course you won't play the Queen Bee, that wouldn't be you.' She grabbed Cassie's arms and shook them. 'Don't forget, you *are* still you.'

'I hope you're right.'

Isabella ignored her. 'Hey, you can invite me to the oh-so-sacred common room. And extra time off for being Few means more time on Madison Avenue.'

'How did I know you'd work shopping into this somehow?' Cassie said, a genuine smile finally crossing her lips. She purposefully stood up and stretched. 'Come on, let's get dressed and find some breakfast. It'll take me at least an hour to look as good as you look right now. And let me tell you, you don't look great.'

Isabella threw a pillow at her. 'Swine. Anyway, it isn't true. You look very beautiful since you had your famous "solution". But wait till you start feeding on me!' She preened, licking a fingertip and smoothing an eyebrow.

Cassie managed to laugh. Taking hold of Isabella's ankle, she started to drag her out of bed. 'Let's get going, girl. You can't avoid Herr Stolz for ever, you know.'

'True.' Isabella threw off her bedclothes and jumped to her feet, pouting. 'But with my powerful new roommate, I was hoping I could.'

Cassie giggled. 'We all have our problems. I get to be possessed by a demon, you get to face the deadly algebraic equations of the maths master.'

'You know, Cassie?' Isabella sighed. 'I'm not sure which is worse . . .'

CHAPTER FIVE

Cassie remembered all too clearly the way she'd felt at the beginning of last term, the fish-out-of-water awfulness of it. She must have looked a bit like a fish, too, if the handful of new students were anything to go by – all wide eyes and gaping mouths. She smothered a smile, feeling sorry for them, but a little superior too. She wasn't the hopeless newbie any more: it was *almost* as if she belonged here. And that felt nice, it really did.

She'd lost Isabella in the throng of students in the atrium, excitedly squealing greetings and indulging in excitable one-upmanship about holidays in exotic locales. As she made her way towards Herr Stolz's classroom, Cassie noticed at least one familiar face of her own. Jake was standing near a bank of sleek lockers with electronic keypads. He looked slightly nervous as Cassie approached.

'Hey, Jake! How's it going?'

'Uh, hey, Cassie. I'm OK, how are you? Feeling better today?' He reached over and gave her an awkward hug, and Cassie felt her heart sink. It had taken months for her and Jake to overcome their mutual wariness. Then, just as they had become real friends, events had taken over. Now, as well as being a walking reminder of his lost sister, Cassie was also one of the Few – part of the group responsible for Jessica's death. No wonder there was tension between them; his feelings towards her must be almost as mixed up as her own. She only hoped she'd be able to show Jake that he could still trust her – and prove it to herself . . .

As they made their way into the classroom, Cassie's attention was drawn to a pale, nervous red-headed girl who had dropped her maths books outside the glass door. A tall boy appeared slickly at her side. He crouched down to help, touching the redhead's elbow in a way that sent a visible shiver through the poor creature. She gazed at him awestruck as he passed her books into her arms, and finally Cassie caught sight of his face. Foppishly handsome, with a dazzling grin.

Richard Halton-Jones.

Cassie felt cold. Obviously he hadn't changed: still an incorrigible flirt. Show him someone – anyone – that walked upright on two legs and he just couldn't help himself. She'd once thought it was endearing; now the memory of their last encounter felt like a punch in the stomach. She'd liked him, trusted him, even started to believe that he was interested in her too, and look where that had got her. Richard was the one who'd lured her to the Arc de Triomphe and a ceremony she'd wanted no part of. She didn't care that it was at the request of the elderly Madame Azzedine, who had taken a shine to Cassie, and deemed her the perfect new host. If it weren't for him, she wouldn't be in this mess.

Averting her eyes sharply, she edged past Richard and into the classroom, hoping he wouldn't take any notice of her. After all, he was lucky he hadn't been expelled. Surely even someone that brazen must be ashamed to be around her after what he had done . . .

Apparently not. A hand squeezed her arm, halting her in her tracks.

'You have no idea,' he murmured, 'how different you look.'

She spun on her heel to glare at him.

Around them, the last students were rushing into class, still loud with gossip and the excitement of a new term, but Herr Stolz was now standing at the front of the room, clearing his throat, tapping his fingers on the desk.

Richard ignored him. 'Hello, Cassie.'

'Class is starting,' she said crisply.

He ignored that as well. 'You look . . . amazing.'

'Thanks.' Her voice was arctic.

'Ah. You sound different, too.'

Was she imagining it, or was that a touch of sadness in his voice? Who cared? Turning away, she saw Isabella breeze into the classroom and fling herself at Jake, almost toppling his seat over. That raised a smile, though Cassie noticed that Jake, who had been scribbling furiously in a notebook, still looked a little distracted. Cassie frowned – after all the time it had taken for Isabella to win him over, she'd have hoped Jake would pay her best friend a little more attention. She slid into a seat next to the pair.

'Steady on, Isabella! You'll damage the furniture.'

'Ah, Cassie! There you are! Fear not, Jake's manly body is sturdy enough to hold little old me.' Isabella fluttered her eyelashes at her boyfriend, who finally put down his pen and swiftly kissed her nose.

Surveying the room properly for the first time, Cassie realised that the sleek, modern desks and chairs were probably too well-made to give way in any case. They were fantastically stylish compared with the traditional wooden furniture that had filled the Academy back in Paris. In fact, they looked as if they'd been carved from lumps of blue ice by Phillipe Starck himself.

'Cassie!'

She turned to see where the call had come from, and found herself staring at a small clique sitting at the back of the classroom, slightly apart from their fellow students. Some of them seemed to regard her with loathing, some with cautious smiles, but all were, without exception, stunningly good-looking.

The Few. Her new 'family'.

Ayeesha and her Irish boyfriend Cormac, two of the more friendly-looking, waved enthusiastically. The Bajan girl called her name again and beckoned her towards an empty desk next to where they were sitting. Ayeesha looked genuinely welcoming, and didn't make Cassie's antennae tingle the way some of the others did. Surely she hadn't been one of the dark, hooded figures at the Arc de Triomphe ceremony. Surely . . . Remembering the sinister horror, Cassie shivered.

'I think you're being summoned,' Jake said, his dry humour not quite covering the note of disdain in his voice.

Cassie averted her eyes hurriedly. 'Don't be daft. I'm not going over there. I'm sitting with you guys, same as always.'

'Ah, we are *honoured*, Ms Bell!' A mischievous singsong lilt was in Isabella's voice, but Cassie's sideways look stopped her short. The last thing she needed was to give the impression that she wanted to be treated differently now, especially around Jake – she was already wary of his feelings towards her.

Cassie nudged Jake and forced herself to smile. 'Oh, *I* get it. You want to get rid of the third wheel so you can have Isabella all to yourself, eh?'

Jake chuckled and held up his hands in mock protest, but his grin quickly faded as he glanced at someone approaching behind her. 'I think we have the full complement of wheels,' he muttered, turning away.

'Is this seat taken?'

Cassie looked up sharply and her heartbeat broke into a sprint.

'Ranjit!' Cassie felt her face redden at the undisguised enthusiasm in her voice. 'Um, hi. No, it's not taken.'

'Can we come to order, please?' At the front of the classroom Herr Stolz was attempting, with little success, to exert his authority. 'Welcome back, all of you. Mr Singh, if you could take a seat, please? We must begin.'

Ranjit nodded a nonchalant apology in Herr Stolz's direction before sliding elegantly into the chair beside her. Isabella looked at Cassie and giggled; Jake remained silent and unsmiling. Ignoring the low ripples of surprise surrounding her (maybe not everyone in the school had seen their clinch in the atrium after all), Cassie opened her textbook and smoothed down its pages carefully. She flushed as Ranjit half-turned his head to her and smiled.

A tingle on the back of her neck told her that more eyes were upon her. She glanced quickly up and turned in her seat, expecting to find half of the Few drilling daggers into her back.

So it was a surprise to meet only Richard's steady, miserable gaze.

Richard must have got some of his *joie de vivre* back over the course of the lesson, cheered by his own good-natured taunting of the hyper-serious teacher. When he approached Cassie at the bell while Ranjit was delayed by Herr Stoltz, he was all charm once more.

'You're angry with me. You're angry with me! Cassie, sweet girl, I can't bear it. I shall kill myself. No, I shall throw myself on the streets. I shall sell my body for a few groats and die, pale and thin, in a garret. I shall waste away. I shall write desperate, terrible poetry. I shall—'

'Shut up, Richard.' Cassie turned away, adjusting the heavy pile of books in her arms as she peered through the jostling students, trying to catch sight of Isabella and Jake. They were already out in the corridor and all wrapped up in one another. She glanced around for

Ranjit, but now he was speaking to his roommate, a lean Danish boy called Torvald.

'For you, darling, I'll shut up,' Richard said smoothly.

'In my dreams. In *everyone's* dreams.'

'I'm still in your dreams?' He clasped his hands to his heart, mock-swooning.

Cassie scowled, cross with herself. If she got drawn into his silly banter there was a chance she'd forgive him. And he didn't deserve to be forgiven. 'Bugger off, Richard. I mean it. Surely you must realise that your little act is totally wasted on me now.' Cassie walked deliberately away towards Isabella, stopping at her roommate's side with a feeling of vicious satisfaction. Richard was left standing in the doorway; she could see his reflection in the glass, looking lost and genuinely wounded. Good.

The thought of Richard was banished from her mind by a jolt of electricity as Ranjit returned and placed one hand gently on the small of her back. Ayeesha and Cormac followed closely behind him. A little reluctantly, Cassie turned to them and smiled. 'Hi, guys.'

'Hey, Cassie, Ranjit,' called Ayeesha as she approached. She turned to Ranjit and nodded with obvious respect. Cassie still didn't have a full grasp on the hierarchy of the Few, but there was no doubt who was top dog. A little thrill of power went through her at the thought that she was dating him. A smile twitched at Ranjit's lips, as though he knew what she was thinking.

'Don't wander off,' continued Ayeesha. 'Come up to the common room. We should show you around, Cassie.'

'We're going there now, thought we'd skip English lit,' added Cormac.

Cassie took a breath. In spite of Isabella's obvious interest, she'd been half-hoping she could avoid the Common Room: the elite, exclusive, sacrosanct common room of the Few . . .

'Uh, well, I have a free period now, so I thought I could catch up on a bit of unpacking and stuff. And I don't know about cutting class . . .'

'Oh, don't worry about that. Come on! Come and meet the others. Have a chat. Get to know us all.'

Was she anywhere near ready for this? For small talk with people she might last have seen behind red hoods, chaining her down at the mercy of Estelle Azzedine? She didn't even know which ones they were . . .

'Go on, Cassie!' Isabella chimed in, jiggling her arm. 'It sounds like fun.'

Jake looked thunderous. His silence spoke volumes for Cassie, and she opened her mouth to decline the offer. But just then, three sixth-form girls swept past towards the atrium. One of them – Sara, was it? – shot her a supercilious glance and muttered something *sotto voce* to her friends, prompting a fit of giggling. Cassie couldn't make out exactly what was said, but she'd distinctly heard the word *common*, and she was pretty sure they weren't talking about the room.

Sara was Few, Cassie knew that. Did her eyes look familiar? Had she seen those cool, grey-blue irises through a slit in a red hood? Rage rose up in her. There was only one way to find out . . .

'You know what?' Cassie told Ayeesha loudly. 'Actually, that'd be great. I'll come along later on this afternoon.'

'Great! See you then.'

As Ayeesha and Cormac walked off, Cassie's heart sank. She regretted being so impulsive. She really wasn't ready to face the common room. Cassie eyed Jake self-consciously as Ranjit turned to her and took her hand.

'I've got a couple of things I need to take care of too. But I'll come and meet you after your English class and we can head up there together.'

Cassie smiled as she watched him stride gracefully away. How did he know exactly the right thing to say? With Ranjit at her side, the common room suddenly wasn't such a daunting prospect.

'Ugh. Socialising with the chosen ones. I can't wait.'

'Cassie! What did I tell you about looking on the bright

side? Embrace the good things! If I had the chance to skip boring old English lit, I would have jumped in it!' Isabella dug her elbow into Cassie's ribs.

'Ouch! Jeez, Isabella!'

'So . . . you and Singh are making a go of it, huh?' Jake said, his voice tight. Cassie could tell he was about as keen to ask that question as she was to answer it. She shuffled along beside them, keeping her eyes on her battered trainers.

'Uh, yeah. I know it's a bit awkward, but he's one of the good guys, Jake. I'm certain of it.'

'Well, I'm glad *you* are.'

Isabella glared at Jake. 'I mean, I guess you're probably right,' he hastily qualified.

But he didn't look at Cassie as he spoke. She knew that he had long suspected Ranjit of having killed his sister. Even Katerina's confession that she and Keiko had committed the crime hadn't been enough to convince Jake that Ranjit wasn't in some way responsible. And Cassie had to admit there were still unanswered questions. Ranjit had been due to meet Jess the night she was killed, but Katerina had sent someone to delay him. Who had that been, and how much did they know about the plot? Cassie wasn't sure she wanted to find out – and even if she did, she had a feeling Ranjit wouldn't say.

Jessica Johnson. The dead girl felt like the elephant in the room in so many of her relationships, sometimes it was almost as though she was still alive and there at the Academy . . .

'Jake—' Cassie began.

He shook his head and nudged her good-naturedly. 'Hey, ignore me. I'm sorry. I've not quite forgiven or forgotten yet, I guess. But I'm here, and that's something. Anyway, we're under instructions from this beautiful girl here to lighten up. Sorry, baby,' he said, putting his arm around Isabella's shoulders as they made their way down the hall.

'No problem,' Isabella said, glowing at his compliment.

Jake cleared his throat, and moved swiftly on to another topic Cassie wasn't keen to discuss.

'So anyway, when am I going to find out what happened in Darke's office, huh? I want to know what he said. What did you do, Cassie? What did *he* do?'

'Um . . .'

'You look a hell of a lot better now, that's for sure. Was it something to do with, uh, feeding?' Jake's voice was casual, but it couldn't quite hide the urgency behind his question, and Cassie began to worry he'd jumped to the right conclusion. 'Come on, what happened? Fess up.' He attempted a smile.

Cassie glanced at Isabella and noticed the very slight shake of her head. Taking a deep breath, she once again couldn't quite meet Jake's eye. 'Sir Alric gave me a shot of something. Kind of a drug. But not a drug.'

Jake stayed silent for an agonising moment. At last he said, 'A drug?'

'Yeah. Not dangerous or anything. It's something the Few can take. To ward off the hunger.' That wasn't a lie, after all.

'Oh.' He looked dumbfounded. 'So, the feeding thing?'

'I just got the injection, and . . . now it's all fine.' Behind her back, Cassie crossed the fingers of both hands.

'Really?' Jake frowned, and then made a face. 'Well, that's great. Why the hell didn't you tell me? It seems pretty straightforward. God, you had me worried there, you know, with what Keiko did and all.'

'Yeah. No. I mean, I'm fine now.' Cassie could barely raise a smile. Guilt twisted her gut.

He smiled ruefully back. 'Well, I'm glad you're OK, anyhow.'

'Uh, cheers.'

'Right,' harrumphed Isabella, a nervous note in her voice. 'Are you happy now, Jake?'

Her boyfriend grinned and gave her a faux-meek nod.

'Then I need to talk to Cassie.' She wagged a finger at

Jake and linked arms with her roommate. 'Alone!'

'Hey, what can't I hear?' he asked plaintively.

Isabella let go of Cassie's arm and wrapped herself around Jake's neck. She planted an enthusiastic kiss on his lips then pulled away. 'Girl talk.'

It seemed to convince him. He raised his hands in defeat. 'OK. In that case, I'm *definitely* going. See you later, girls.'

Isabella grinned and waved him goodbye.

When he'd disappeared from sight, Cassie exhaled deeply. 'I feel like a shit,' she muttered.

Isabella clasped her hand. 'Thank you, Cassie.'

'For what? Lying to him?'

'For being discreet. I don't want him to know about the feeding. It will bring back too many painful memories of Jess.'

Cassie let Isabella precede her into the elevator. 'He's got to know eventually.'

'Yes,' conceded Isabella miserably. 'But not yet, hmm?'

'The longer we leave it . . .'

'The longer he'll be happy. Ignorance is blissful, isn't it? So let's not tell him just yet.'

'OK,' sighed Cassie as the elevator door slid silently open at their floor. 'But I want a favour for keeping my mouth shut.'

Isabella slipped her arm through Cassie's. 'Name it! A polo pony?'

Cassie giggled. 'As if. All I want is a shot on your laptop, to check my emails and stuff?'

'Ooh, you ask so *much*.' Isabella tossed her hair dramatically, then laughed. Sweeping into their room and flinging her bag on to her bed, she patted her laptop. 'There you go!'

Cassie logged on, found her webmail folder and scrolled down through the messages. A couple of emails from the kids back at Cranlake, including some really bad jokes which made her laugh out loud. Otherwise nothing but special offers from websites she'd visited. Boring.

There was one more. Although she was expecting it, the sender's name on the last message in the folder hit her with a jolt. With a flush of guilt, she took a deep breath.

From: Patrick Malone

Subject: Fw: Fw: How's things?

Give the man his due, he was persistent. He had sent the same email three times now, with minor variations. How was New York? How was the flight? Was she OK? He hadn't heard from her – was something wrong? Could she just reply to this, or better yet call him, so he'd know she was OK? Cassie, could you *please* just acknowledge this? How are you feeling?

She sighed. How was she feeling? Not ready to talk. Definitely not ready to confront what had happened at Christmas, or what Patrick might know . . .

Gently she stroked the touchpad, guiding the cursor to the delete button.

Delete this message?

Hesitating only for a moment, she clicked 'Yes'.

CHAPTER SIX

Cassie took a deep breath. It seemed a daring act of sacrilege just to touch the beautiful inlaid common-room door. The patterns were so intricate, so delicate, she was afraid she might break the wood.

But let's face it: that wasn't why she was hesitating. She eyed Ranjit nervously as he stepped forward and placed his hand on the gleaming silver handle.

'Relax. It'll be fun,' he murmured, reaching down with his other hand to take her own. She rolled her eyes and tried to smile. Ranjit turned the handle and the door swung open.

As they walked in, Cassie took a breath. Why had she been expecting the same Parisian common room, with its antiques and dark fabrics, jewelled lamps and glassware? This vast space, only a floor below Sir Alric's penthouse office, was flooded with light from its glass walls and the frosty blue sky beyond. The leather sofas were clean-lined and ivory-white; the furniture was sleek and minimalist but visibly expensive. Her trainers squeaked on a pale hardwood floor as they crossed the room under stares that ranged from surprised to friendly to violently hostile.

'Hey, you two!' Cormac leaped to his feet, and Ayeesha gave them one of her radiant grins. 'Good to see you both. Come along in and meet the others, Cassie.'

It was extraordinary, she thought, the way the big clique that was the Few was split into its own small but very intense sub-cliques. The people she'd expect to be together were together, classified by personality and general niceness – or lack thereof. The bond between certain Few members, and the division between certain Few groups, was invisible but obvious. They were like small galaxies revolving around each other but never touching. Between some groups, the air almost vibrated with tension. She got the distinct sense, too, that some of the members of each group deferred to the others in a way that seemed to be nothing to do with age.

Whatever the reason for the divisions, all of the room's inhabitants were temporarily united in watching Cassie and Ranjit, and eyeing their clasped hands with interest. Unconcerned, Cormac was gesturing expansively round the room. '. . . and Sara, of course. And you'll know

69

Vassily and India from last term, and Yusuf. Sorry, I'm sure Ranjit can introduce you, I suppose you don't need me to tell you all this.' He gave a warm chuckle. Cassie smiled back, ever-so-slightly beginning to loosen up.

Then the common-room door opened again, and she immediately stiffened with tension once more. The voice she heard calling an elaborate greeting to a group of students in the corner was horribly familiar.

Richard.

Startled, Cassie glanced over at him: how could it have slipped her mind that he would most likely be in the common room? Maybe she'd wilfully forgotten. As their eyes met, he doffed an invisible hat, smiling tentatively, but thankfully saying nothing. Ranjit eyed him warily.

Cormac had returned to flop down on a plush sofa beside Ayeesha, and Cassie sighed deeply. 'OK, that's that experience over. Can we go now?' she whispered through gritted teeth, though a smile pulled at the corners of her mouth.

Ranjit looked down at her tense face and laughed infectiously. His gaze held hers, and Cassie found herself rooted to the spot, calmed by his intense stare. She stared back at him, mesmerised, until, almost in slow motion, Ranjit wrapped his arms around her and pressed his lips to hers. Time seemed to stand still as she melted into his kiss, forgetting her reservations until a loud cough nearby abruptly made her very aware that they were still standing in the middle of the room. Eyes were turned in their direction again. Cormac seemed quietly amused; Richard looked stricken.

'Not again,' she mumbled, grinning sheepishly. 'Aren't we, uh, a little on display here?'

'Oh. Of course, let's, um . . .' Ranjit shook his head a little as if to clear it, and guided her to another plush sofa tucked into a corner of the room. As they went, a burst of good-natured laughter rang out from Richard's group, but Richard didn't seem to be sharing the joke. His eyes were still on Cassie, filled with some undefinable emotion. Then they reached the sofa and sat down, Ranjit put his arm casually around her shoulders, and her heart floated.

Forcing Richard's expression out of her head, Cassie cleared her throat. 'I admit it. This is kind of cool.' She lowered her voice. 'And I'm glad to see they seem just as shocked to see you here as they do me.' She prodded Ranjit's side playfully. He flushed, and Cassie was surprised to see that he looked a little embarrassed.

'I guess so.'

'How come?' Cassie gave him a puzzled look.

'After Jess died, I kept my distance from the rest of the Few. I knew one of them must have been responsible, but

I didn't know who. I suspected all of them. I hardly came to the common room at all last year. It made it kind of hard to have close friendships. And they're wary of me for other reasons.'

'Such as?'

Ranjit sighed. 'The Few respect power – it's how we define ourselves. And I'm strong, Cassie. One of the strongest of the Few at the Academy. I make people nervous – or jealous.'

With a smile, Cassie reached up and ran her fingers through his jet-black hair. 'You're telling me,' she said. He gave a quiet laugh. 'How do they know you're so powerful anyway? How can they tell?'

Ranjit looked at her quizzically. 'Don't you see it?' he asked.

Cassie shrugged. 'Nope.'

'Try. Look at the others now. Let yourself sense their strength.'

Trying not to be too obvious, Cassie shifted in her seat so she could see the rest of the room. 'What do I do?'

'Just relax. Open your mind and it'll happen.'

Feeling intensely awkward, Cassie stared at her classmates. For a moment, nothing happened. Then, slowly, she began to discern a glow that seemed to come from within each of them. A ball of light that hovered around where their heart would be. 'They're beautiful,' she breathed.

'It's the Few spirits,' whispered Ranjit into her ear. 'The brighter the light, the stronger the spirit.'

Some of the lights glowed softly, others burned more powerfully. Cormac's light was low and steady, but Ayeesha's was as bright as a spotlight. The Bajan girl had to be seriously powerful. Casting her eyes over the rest of the room, Cassie could suddenly see that the group divisions were almost all to do with power.

Yusuf, his spirit almost as bright as Ayeesha's, was surrounded by a trio of less powerful Few, as if they were relying on him for patronage and protection. In the far corner, a group of much weaker lights had gathered together, almost like they were seeking safety in numbers. Richard was among them, and Cassie was surprised to see that the English boy's spirit was little more than a candle flame. Odd, she had always figured him for a big player among the Few . . .

'Now look at me,' murmured Ranjit, and his velvety tones brought Cassie's attention back to him. Her breath caught in her throat as she saw his dazzling spirit. It blazed from his chest like a fallen star, eclipsing all others in the room.

Or almost all.

Glancing down, Cassie saw for the first time the glow from her own body – as bright as Ranjit's, it seemed, but different. Rather than being concentrated in her chest, her own light seemed somehow diffuse. As she reached out to touch his face, she could see an aura surrounding her arm, like a halo. Shaking her head, she let the vision fade.

'I'm different,' she said quietly.

Ranjit took her hand. 'You're perfect.'

Cassie felt her heart skip a beat. She smiled back at him shyly. 'If you say so.'

'So now you've seen them as they truly are,' grinned Ranjit. 'Maybe it *would* be good to get to know some of them better. There are actually some decent people among the Few, y'know.'

She leaned forward and skimmed his lips mischievously with her own. Something about his gaze was like a magnet; she couldn't seem to keep her hands off him.

'I know there are,' she whispered pointedly.

'Well, if you change your mind on that, at least you're a little fond of the indecent ones too.'

'Huh?' Cassie frowned.

Ranjit nodded towards Richard, now lounging alone on a corner sofa flicking through a copy of the *National Enquirer*.

'What do you mean, I'm fond of him?' She pulled back a little, bristling.

'Well, he never stopped flirting with you from August to December—'

'Oh, and that's my fault, is it?'

Ranjit stiffened, his eyes suddenly narrowing. 'No, but you've hardly taken your eyes off him since we came in.'

Does he think we don't want him? We do! Cassandra, you must convince him!

Cassie froze at the reappearance of the all-too-familiar voice inside her mind. Beside her, Ranjit's hand slipped out from behind her neck as he turned to face her. 'Come on, Cassie. It's pretty obvious he's interested in you. And you *did* like him. I barely had a look-in last term, until you—'

'Huh!' she interrupted, incredulous. 'I liked him fine, till he tricked me into hosting some goddamn demon.'

And we thank him for that, my dear!

Cassie squeezed her eyes shut for a moment, trying to ignore Estelle's interjections. The old bag had been quiet since the nightmare, why was she back now?

Ranjit's eyes flashed. 'Demon? Is that what you think? What does that make me, then?'

'Ranjit, why are you being like this?' Cassie hissed, turning her body to square up to him more fully. He

75

glowered back for a moment, then, with a deep breath, his look softened. He reached over and touched her knee.

'I'm sorry, Cassie. I didn't mean to . . .' Ranjit lowered his voice. 'Look, I'm sorry. Maybe now's not the time to talk about it.'

Cassie slewed her gaze left and right. Sure enough, a few of the smirks had returned now that she and Ranjit had raised their voices to each other. Taking a deep breath of her own, she slid her arm hesitantly back through Ranjit's.

'OK . . . What if I just forgive you, then?'

'Great. What if I just don't mention Richard Halton-Jones again?'

'Even better.' Cassie gave him a slow grin. Setting her jaw, she decided to put the whole episode behind her. 'Anyway . . . what's happening today in the world of the Few?'

'I think the plan is to watch a movie. Fancy it?'

'Yeah, sure.'

Just as she spoke, one of the older students nearby lifted a remote control and blinds began to slide down the massive windows. With a click and a hum, a huge screen began to descend from the ceiling and the state-of-the-art projector lit up.

'OK, definitely cool,' she said, awed. 'Maybe this

common room thing isn't so bad after all.'

As the lights dimmed, Cassie relaxed into the soft leather of the sofa, trying to forget the image of Ranjit's face, eyes narrowed, jealous and so quick to bridle. She'd never seen that side to him before. They obviously still had a lot to learn about each other. Anyway, wasn't she glad he was jealous? In a way it was nice. Reassuring. Had she overreacted? Was she wrong to have bitten his head off? Probably. But it was only a minor squabble, and he seemed to have forgotten it already.

Sighing, she closed her eyes. The cosy darkness enveloped her, and after a moment, she forgot the film – forgot most things – as she found herself concentrating only on Ranjit's closeness. The intoxicating smell of his body through his shirt. The rise and fall of his chest as he breathed. She felt her fingers clutch his tightly. If she stopped over-analysing everything, she might even forget her worries altogether . . .

CHAPTER SEVEN

Cassie swore under her breath and considered for the fifth time whether hurling her monitor through a seventeenth-floor window would be considered grounds for expulsion.

At the start of term, the new computer science teacher Mr Jackson had seemed a soft touch. But now, a few weeks in, he'd turned into a monster. Their latest project – designing a new section of the Darke Academy website – could have been fun as well as interesting, had Mr Jackson not insisted on including such a complex sequence of animations and graphics. Cassie had always been a dab hand at web design, but she was sick of the sight of Dreamweaver. Her own dreams were trouble enough.

Estelle's nocturnal visits were getting more frequent – three in the last week – and although there had been no repeat of the melting photo frame incident, Cassie couldn't shake the notion that the two events were somehow connected. She had considered asking Ranjit about them, but she knew that he found it disturbing that Cassie could hear Estelle's voice, and she didn't want to make him uncomfortable.

Cassie sighed, refocusing on the screen in front of her. Perhaps Jake could help – the boy seemed glued to his laptop these days, whether in or out of class. She'd never had him pegged as a computer geek, but maybe . . .

She slipped out of her chair and hurried silently across the room, keeping low to avoid the roaming gaze of Mr Jackson.

'Hey, Jake, can you—'

'Cassie!'

Jake practically jumped out of his skin. Flushing red, he scrambled to minimise the window on his screen, but not before Cassie's astonished eyes had caught the words stamped across the top of the page.

THE DARKE ACADEMY STUDENT RECORDS – CONFIDENTIAL

'Jake, what was that?' demanded Cassie.

'Hell, Cassie,' Jake replied, trying to laugh it off. 'You gave me a shock and a half.'

'You're supposed to be designing the front page, not

hacking into the school records system.' Cassie sighed in exasperation as she tugged the mouse from his hands. 'What are you doing anyway? Trying to fiddle your chemistry grades?'

'Hey, don't—' protested Jake. 'Aw, Cassie . . .' He threw up his hands in disgust as Cassie pulled open the window.

Her stomach turned a backflip. She turned to Jake, but he was staring at the tabletop and wouldn't meet her eye.

'Jake, do you have any idea how much trouble you could get into for doing this?' Cassie demanded. 'This is Katerina's personal file! What the hell are you playing at?'

'Just leave it, Cassie. It's none of your business.'

'None of my business? She tried to kill me, remember?'

Jake's eyes blazed. 'Yeah, well she *did* kill my sister. Remember that? Did you think I was just gonna let that go?'

'Jake, we've been through this—'

'She admitted it, Cassie! She told us she killed her, and she *laughed*. And all Darke did was expel her. Is that fair? Well, maybe it is for the Few, but I don't subscribe to their idea of justice.'

Cold fear clutched at Cassie's bowels. 'You're not thinking of going looking for her, are you, Jake? Tell me you're not.'

'Ask me no questions, Cassie, I'll tell you no lies.'

'Jake, listen to me.' Cassie struggled to keep her voice as reasonable as she could. 'Promise me that you'll stop this. Please. We both know that Katerina killed Jess, but there's no way of proving it, even if you find her.'

Jake sighed bitterly. 'At this moment, I'd settle for just finding her, Cassie. And that's easier said than done. The address in this file is in Sweden and I've already checked it out. The Svenssons sold the place a month ago and left. No forwarding address.'

Relief swamped her. With the Few's network of connections, surely there was no way Jake could find Katerina if she didn't want to be found.

'Please, Jake. I know it's hard, but you have to let this go.'

Jake's gaze was apologetic. 'I can't, Cassie. I owe it to Jess. I'm going to find Katerina. She's going to be punished for what she did. I swear it.'

'Mr Johnson? Miss Bell? I wasn't aware that you were working on this project together?'

Cassie started at the teacher's voice.

'Um, no . . . sorry, Mr Jackson, I was just asking Jake about editing HTML code,' she mumbled.

'Well, call me traditional, but I think it's usual for questions in class to be directed to the teacher.'

'Yes, sir,' muttered Cassie, gritting her teeth.

'So why don't you come on back to your seat and I'll see if I can help.'

As she made her way across the classroom, Cassie shot a final pleading look at Jake, but he seemed to be concentrating on his own screen. He looked determined. As determined as she'd ever seen him. This was going to be trouble . . .

CHAPTER EIGHT

'You know, I've never had a date in a railway station before,' said Cassie.

Ranjit grinned. 'You don't know what you've been missing.'

No kidding. Cassie was really pleased when Ranjit had suggested a bit of sightseeing together earlier that afternoon. She'd felt as if a distance had opened up between them after their spat in the common room, and Cassie had been hopeful that his suggestion of an afternoon alone could be enough to change that. However, when he brought her to a train station she wasn't quite so sure it was going to be the romantic reconciliation she was hoping for after all.

Luckily, it didn't take long to change her mind when Ranjit led her up to the Oyster Bar. Even with her limited experience of such matters, Cassie had a glimmer of hope that the crustaceans might provide an early-evening aphrodisiac . . .

'Good, aren't they?' Ranjit looked up from under his long, dark lashes and grinned. As he returned to his plate of expensive shellfish, Cassie eyed her fellow diners. The three women at the next table were animated, laughing at some juicy piece of gossip. She watched their mouths, sniffed delicately at the scent of their breath. Their lively auras were almost more appealing than oysters, but she wasn't afraid of attacking them. Not yet. Inside her, the hunger was quiet. The Tears of the Few were still doing their job, thank goodness. She still had time.

'You're all right, aren't you?' Ranjit asked, reaching a hand over to touch hers.

Her skin tingled. 'Absolutely.' As if to prove it, she swallowed another oyster, and leaned contentedly back in her chair. The ceiling above her was stunning: vaulted and tiled and glowing with light. 'What a beautiful place.'

'I know it sounds weird, but the main terminal's even better.' He laughed. 'Are you finished? I'll get the bill and we can go upstairs.' Dropping his napkin on the red checked tablecloth, he nodded to a waiter. Handing over a shiny black credit card, he paid without checking the amount. Cassie gave a short, private laugh. The casual wealth of the students at the Darke Academy never ceased to amaze her.

Ranjit walked around and helped her into her coat, and

she smiled as he rested his hands on her shoulders for a fraction longer than necessary.

'Hey, is everything cool with you and Jake?'

Cassie hesitated, surprised at his question – and on guard after what had happened when he'd brought up the subject of Richard. 'Yeah. Why wouldn't it be?'

'I don't know. I just haven't seen him hanging out with you as much as usual recently. I know he's not exactly thrilled with the idea of us being together. And after what happened to Jess, I can't imagine he's happy about you feeding on Isabella either.'

Cassie silently cursed his perceptiveness. Jake had indeed been keeping his distance since their 'chat' in computer science. But how much could she tell Ranjit? She wasn't ready to let anyone else know about Jake's one-man campaign to bring Katerina to justice, that was for sure.

She bought a little time by knotting her scarf carefully. At last she gave Ranjit an apologetic grin. 'Yeah, you have a point. Things have been a bit . . . tense. But actually, he doesn't know about the feeding thing yet.'

He raised his eyebrows. 'Really? Well, maybe that's for the best. But how long do you think you can keep it from him? Jake isn't stupid.'

'I know.' Cassie made a rueful face. 'But we haven't

actually done anything yet, so it's not like we're actually lying. And Isabella really, really doesn't want him to know.'

'Yeah. I can believe that,' Ranjit said. 'Still, that's a pretty amazing friend you've got there.'

'She's very brave,' Cassie replied quietly. 'Braver than I'd be. Anyway, we've got an appointment with Sir Alric tomorrow. Isabella and me. He's going to give us our first . . . um, tutorial.'

'Good. It will be much easier for you to get used to the idea of being one of us once you're surer about the feeding.'

She shifted uncomfortably at his choice of phrase. 'One of us'. The reminder that Ranjit was as much a member of the Few as those sinister figures who had lurked, hooded, in the shadows during her ritual. He had spoken a little about the dark nature of the spirit inside him, the 'personality clash' they had – a bad spirit in a good person. Like Cassie and Estelle, perhaps. Was she falling for a monster?

Was *he*?

Of course not, my dear . . .

Cassie tensed. As they walked towards the stairs, Ranjit sensed her discomfort.

'Cassie . . . I know things are a little different for you, and it's going to take some getting used to, but I promise you, it's not all bad.'

'That's easy for you to say – you don't have *your* spirit interrupting your thoughts at random intervals.' She turned and gave him a half-hearted smile, but couldn't keep it up. She was suddenly on a downer.

'I mean, you've got more of a sense of unity, even if you do struggle with your nature. I'm an outsider even amongst the outsiders. And I'm nothing like any of you lot. You're all rich, suave, privileged. I'm a Scholarship, for God's sake, on top of everything else . . .' She trailed off and stopped at the top of the stairs, taking a ragged breath. People brushed past them as they stood facing one another. Ranjit reached over and took both her hands in his.

'You . . .' he leaned in towards her, 'need to stop worrying so much. I may not be able to talk to my spirit, but I'm still on your side. I do have some idea what you're going through. Believe it or not, I don't just breeze through life without a care, despite what you might think.' He seemed to be trying to comfort her, but there was a faint edge to his voice. He paused for a moment, squeezing his eyes shut as if trying to block something out. Without opening them, his lips found hers. Then after what seemed like forever, he pulled away. A small whimper escaped from Cassie's mouth. Or was it just inside her head . . . ?

Finally, wordlessly, he grabbed her hand and guided her down the stairs. For a moment all thoughts of their problems went clean out of her head as they came to a halt.

'Oh, wow,' Cassie breathed.

They were standing in the main concourse of Grand Central Station, below its iconic clock. Around them, commuters and tourists swarmed through the huge space, but she could only stare at the colossal arched windows, the elegant stonework, and most of all, the extravagantly beautiful painted ceiling. Once her attention was caught, she couldn't look away.

She turned, dizzy with staring upwards. 'It's the zodiac.'

'Yes.' Ranjit had his hand on her elbow, steadying her. 'Painted the wrong way round. See?'

'I wouldn't know. Is it?'

'By mistake, yes. The Vanderbilt family commissioned the work early last century. When the error was spotted, they said it was deliberate. They said it's as if we're looking down on the stars. A God's-eye view.'

Slowly, Cassie turned around again, taking it in. 'I like that,' she murmured. 'A God's-eye view. How appropriate.'

'All right, Cassie Bell. So now we've got the first awkward date out of the way . . .'

'Mmm?' Awkward was right.

'Please can I take you out again?' His words rushed out.

'Properly?' His sheepish grin ruined her. 'Valentine's Day?'

Cassie took a breath. She'd never had a real Valentine's date before: in fact, if it hadn't been for the hearts-and-flowers displays in every shop front, she'd have forgotten the day was approaching.

'OK,' she said slowly, suddenly feeling hot.

He cocked an eyebrow, and the expression of mock outrage on his face made her laugh out loud.

'Sorry – yes. Yes, I'd love to.'

'Wonderful!' His smile lit up his whole face, making him look altogether different. Cassie couldn't help wishing she could give him that look more often.

'So am I allowed to ask where we're going?'

'No, absolutely not. It's a surprise.'

'Great.' She squeezed his arm mischievously. 'It's not as if I've had enough of those.'

'Ha ha. Hey, it's still pretty early. Want to go and take a look at the trains?'

She slipped her hand into his as they moved through the hurrying crowds. 'So, what have we got here? Thomas? Percy? The Hogwarts Express?'

He laughed and squeezed her fingers. 'Bog-standard Metro-North trains. But you never know. Keep your eyes peeled.'

They walked slowly, taking in the sight of thousands of

New Yorkers and tourists. She took a moment to just enjoy being with Ranjit, and not being in a hurry to go anywhere. 'It's like a dance. How can this many people never bump into each other?'

'I never thought of it that way. You're right, it is pretty amazing. What else can we do here? Do you want to take a look at the shopping concourse?'

'Ha! I get enough of that with Isabella!' Cassie chuckled, over the whistle of a train about to depart.

'I confess, that's a relief.'

Letting go of Ranjit's hand, Cassie backed away and looked upwards, craning her neck. 'Who'd believe a railway station could be this entertaining?'

'Well, you know, they nearly demolished— CASSIE!'

Out of nowhere, a figure was sprinting towards the departing train, shouldering Cassie violently aside. Taken completely by surprise, she stumbled sideways with a cry of shock.

She was aware of a train pulling in, of the deafening noise of it as she teetered on the edge of the platform, and the high shriek of what might have been a whistle or a terrified onlooker. Her arms flailed wildly in the air as she fell towards the track.

Then Ranjit snatched hold of her, his iron grasp dragging her desperately back to safety. As he clutched her wrist and finally pulled her clear, she felt the rush of wind in her hair from the train, the solid platform under her feet, and the tight grip of Ranjit's arms.

'It's fine. She's fine. Thanks.' Pale with shock, he waved away a few concerned commuters, and in seconds they were left alone, the crowds once more sweeping past. Cassie could feel his muscles trembling beneath his coat.

'Thanks, Sir Galahad.' Her voice shook.

'Jeez, that was close.' Ranjit held her tighter. 'Who was that idiot?'

'Dunno. Bloody New Yorkers. Late for a meeting, I guess.' Cassie managed to choke out a laugh.

The train the figure had caught was pulling away. Ranjit gave it a last glare, then hugged Cassie again. 'Are you sure you're OK?'

'Yeah. Honestly.' She shivered, and he pulled her coat tighter around her.

'Know what? I think we've had enough sightseeing for today.'

'I agree. Railway stations, eh? Entertaining, but dangerous too.' She smiled shakily. 'Let's go back.'

CHAPTER NINE

Cassie didn't sleep well that night. Every time she began to drop off, she'd feel the rush of the train, hear the shriek of its whistle. And in the uneasy half-dreams, there were no hands to seize her and pull her away – instead *she* reached out, pulling Ranjit down with her. In the dreams, she just kept on falling, falling, Estelle's voice ringing in her ears . . .

Yet again, she started awake, breathing hard. It was still night outside, but she fumbled for her watch and peered at it in the faint city glow. She groaned. Feeling hopelessly sleep-deprived, she swung her legs out of bed for fear of falling back into a doze. That would be just typical.

'Time to get up. Hey, partner. Wakey, wakey.'

Isabella snored on until Cassie pummelled her awake, and then she tried to burrow back under the covers. 'Cassie, no . . .'

'Cassie, *yes*. Get up, girl. We have to go and see Sir Alric, remember?'

'Tomorrow. It can wait till tomorrow . . .'

'It *is* tomorrow, Isabella!'

Finally, Cassie resorted to the tried and tested trick of pulling her roommate out of bed by the ankles. Isabella only woke properly when she thudded to the floor. Cross and bleary, she blinked up at Cassie through her tangled mane, then shoved it out of her eyes.

'Oh, yes. Of course. Sorry. We have an appointment, don't we?'

By the time they were both dressed and heading for Sir Alric's office, Isabella irritatingly seemed almost as bright and breezy as always. If she was feeling tense, she covered it well. It was Cassie who felt heavy with tiredness and brimming with nerves.

As she raised a fist to knock on his door, it opened. Cassie recognised the smiling Few boy who was leaving the office.

'Hi, Paco. Hi, Louis.' Isabella smiled at his roommate behind him.

'Morning!' Paco seemed absurdly lively for the early hour. His eyes fairly sparkled and he glowed with energy. Louis, though, was yawning. He gave Cassie and Isabella a sleepy smile.

'You too, huh?' He rubbed his eyes and shook his head.

'What?' said Cassie.

'Extra Latin tuition first thing. Pain in the derrière, non?'

Cassie could only laugh weakly and nod, but she didn't miss Paco's sly wink, aimed only at her. She ignored him as Sir Alric called them into the room and the door closed on the boys.

'Cassandra. Isabella.' He bestowed reassuring smiles on each of them. 'Thank you for coming.'

'Not really optional, is it?' pointed out Cassie dryly.

Sir Alric gave a brief laugh. 'Isabella, welcome. Cassandra tells me that she has spoken with you about her . . . special needs. And that you have agreed to become her life-source. I take it you're still sure about your decision?'

Isabella smiled tightly. 'Of course.'

'Not many people have the luxury of choice in this matter,' said Sir Alric gravely. 'As you know, most roommates are unaware of the true nature of the Few.'

'Yes, Louis for example?' Isabella interjected, arching an eyebrow disapprovingly. 'He does not know that Paco is feeding from him?'

'No, he does not. But let me assure you that whether or not the life-source is aware of what is happening to them, if it is properly performed, the feeding process is entirely harmless.' Sir Alric gestured towards two large, dark leather chairs. 'Please take a seat, both of you, and I'll do my best to answer any questions you have before we begin.'

He sat opposite them, folding one long leg over the other and regarding them expectantly. Cassie's heart raced – she didn't know where to begin. She glanced over at Isabella, but she seemed at a sudden and uncharacteristic loss for words as well. Sir Alric broke the silence.

'Well, firstly, perhaps it might be useful for you both to think of these sessions in the same manner as any of your other lessons. What we are hoping to achieve here is part of the core aim of the Academy – to prepare our students for life outside these hallowed walls. Indeed, you may wish to think of the Academy itself as a training ground of sorts.'

'Training ground?' Cassie ventured.

'Yes. As you know, here at the Darke Academy we select students that we believe have the potential to be suitable hosts for the Few. The academic setting provides the chosen Few with the opportunity to obtain the skills and personal connections necessary to become leading members of society.'

'And the rest are just here as snacks?' Cassie was becoming less sure about this idea by the second.

'The other students,' continued Sir Alric, unruffled, 'serve a vital role in our world. And by extension, the world at large. In giving of themselves – their life-energy – they help to nurture our future leaders, artists and scientists – individuals vital to humanity. And in return, they are the beneficiaries of an unrivalled, world-class education that will stand them in good stead in their own lives.'

Cassie let out a mirthless laugh. 'Vital to humanity . . . ?' she began, but Isabella leaned forward and held up one hand.

'But why do you have to do it without our consent? And why does each member of the Few have to feed on their roommate, in particular?' she asked, her brow lined with a mixture of curiosity and concern.

Sir Alric steepled his fingers and began again cautiously. 'Over the years, we have found that secrecy is the best policy. Not everyone would be as accepting of the Few as you have been, Isabella. If the world knew the truth about us – about our strengths and skills and what we need to do to maintain them – how long do you think it would be before we found ourselves branded monsters? Feared and persecuted wherever we went. No. There is safety in secrecy, and it is for that reason that most members of the Few choose to keep their roommates ignorant of what is happening to them.'

Isabella nodded.

'As for why we insist that each member of the Few feeds only on their roommate,' continued Sir Alric, 'if the Few were allowed to feed at random, there would be the risk that one student might be fed on by more than one of the Few, losing too much of their life-energy. It is when that happens that feeding can become dangerous. But if each member of the Few only feeds from their roommate, that danger is avoided. It is merely a precaution, another measure of how seriously we take your safety.'

Cassie was shaking her head.

'Is there a problem, Cassandra?'

'You make it sound so easy. But what about Keiko and Alice? What about what happened to Jess, huh? What about the Few who decide that they're not going to follow the rules of your so-called *system*?' She almost spat the last word.

'In any society, there are those who stray from the path of law. When that happens, they are punished.'

Cassie laughed incredulously. Jake's angry words from their computer science lesson rang in her ears. 'So Katerina was punished for killing Jake's sister by being expelled? Call me unreasonable, but that's one case where the punishment doesn't seem to fit the crime.'

Sir Alric unfolded himself from his chair and stood up,

his expression hardening. Cassie felt a pang of fear alongside her anger and nerves.

'I understand your feelings, Cassandra, but we are not here to discuss Katerina Svensson. Her punishment was decided by powers beyond your knowledge and my control. What is more important now is that you are given proper training in how to feed, and monitored to ensure that you do not make the same mistakes she did.'

Sir Alric's tone carried a definite ring of finality. Question time was over.

'Now, I have another appointment shortly, so we should begin. Isabella, if you could please come over here.' Sir Alric gestured to the space in front of him. 'And you here, Cassandra.'

Cassie took up the position indicated in front of Isabella, her palms sweating. Isabella giggled nervously and puckered her lips.

Sir Alric arched a perfect eyebrow. 'What are you doing, Miss Caruso?'

Isabella glanced uneasily between Cassie and Sir Alric. 'Cassie said that when Keiko fed on Alice it was like she was kissing her. So I thought . . .'

'Keiko's method was *not* the manner by which we recommend this process should be undertaken. Her proclivities were cruel, and her decision to feed in that manner merely reflected those proclivities. Direct mouth-to-mouth feeding is more powerful, but also more harmful.'

'Phew! Finally some good news!' Cassie managed to crack a smile. 'No offence, Isabella, but you're not really my type.'

'None taken, darling,' Isabella replied, winking.

Sir Alric smiled as well, then shook his head. 'Let's not get ahead of ourselves. Cassandra, take hold of Isabella's wrist, like so . . .' He demonstrated, wrapping his index finger and thumb tightly around her own wrist. Cassie reached over and did as he said, shuffling her feet uncomfortably.

'So far, so good,' Isabella said, nodding encouragingly to Cassie.

'A little tighter,' said Sir Alric briskly. Cassie tightened her grip on Isabella's wrists, watching her roommate closely. She could feel her pulse underneath her thumbs. Sir Alric continued.

'Now, you must think, all the time, Cassandra. Think about what you are doing, about the importance of it. Think about Isabella as well as yourself. Don't ever let yourself go onto automatic pilot; that's when you'll lose control. Start slowly. Do you understand?'

She nodded, swallowing.

'Now, Isabella – this may feel a little unusual,' said Sir Alric, his voice calm and level. 'But I am here. You have my word that you will not be harmed.'

'OK,' said Isabella, sounding uneasy.

'Are you *sure* you want to go through with this?' asked Cassie.

'Sure. Honestly, Cassie. I trust you.'

'Yeah, but I'm not sure I trust myself,' Cassie mumbled, her mind flying back to Cranlake Crescent and the moment she had attacked Patrick.

'Then I will trust you for both of us.' Isabella's smile was shaky, but her voice was firm.

'Right,' said Sir Alric, putting a hand on Cassie's shoulder. 'Both of you close your eyes.' He paused. 'Now, Cassandra. Take a deep breath and try to relax.'

Cassie did as he said, but nothing seemed to happen.

'Once more. Concentrate.'

Sir Alric's voice faded as Cassie drew a second deep breath. This time there was a change. As she breathed in, her senses seemed somehow to be heightened. Beneath her fingertips, Isabella's pulse was pounding, racing. She could sense the life-energy flowing through her roommate's veins.

'That's it,' murmured Sir Alric.

Now Cassie could feel a prickling sensation all over her

skin, a humming inside her head, a bright glow behind her eyelids. She was at once both light-headed and totally, completely alert, and she realised she was still inhaling, her lungs seemingly no nearer to being filled.

'Concentrate,' came Sir Alric's voice once more, over the buzzing in her head. Cassie slowly opened her eyes, still breathing in, her fingers coiled tightly around Isabella's slender wrists. Blinking, she noticed Isabella's own eyes were squeezed shut, her mouth hanging slightly open, a barely perceptible sigh emitting from her lips, and Cassie instinctively knew that the endless breath coming out of her friend and into her was the life-energy she needed. Filling her with power . . .

Yes, my dear! That's it! Feed me, Cassandra!

With a choking noise, Cassie dropped Isabella's wrists and took a pace backward. Isabella's eyes opened lazily, and she coughed, rubbing her eyelids as though she was trying to wake up from a deep slumber. Cassie's heart was racing, not just out of alarm at what she had been doing, or the reappearance of Estelle's voice, but from the huge, almost overwhelming rush of vitality. She'd never felt more *alive*. It was as though her senses were all snapped into hyper-focus.

'Yes. Good control, Cassandra,' said Sir Alric. Cassie jumped, almost surprised to find he was still standing beside them. 'Well done, both of you.'

Cassie turned to Isabella tentatively. 'Are you OK?'

Isabella paused, then let out a short laugh.

'That's *it*?' Incredulity flooded her voice.

'Isabella? Are you sure you're—'

'I'm absolutely fine,' Isabella said. She looked up at Cassie and grinned, then threw her arms around her friend in a tight hug. 'See, I told you, Cassie Bell. There was no need for all that build-up! No sweat.'

Cassie nodded, still a hint of doubt lingering in her mind.

'Yeah. That was . . . I guess it was less involved than I expected. Still, I don't know if it's something I want to do on a regular basis.' Her head was spinning.

'Regular feeding is a must, Cassie,' said Sir Alric seriously. 'As you have seen, if done properly, it is a simple and harmless procedure. But if you leave it too long – if you let yourself become too hungry – that is when you make mistakes and lose control. And that is when people get hurt.'

He walked to the door and placed a hand on the doorknob. 'For the moment, the Tears of the Few will help to sustain you. As long as their effect lingers, you will not need to feed as regularly as the other Few. You have done well today, but as soon as you feel the hunger growing, Cassandra, you must let me know, and we will meet again.'

Sir Alric Darke opened the door. 'Until then . . .'

CHAPTER TEN

'I look ridiculous.'

'You do *not*. You look gorgeous!'

Cassie and Isabella stood together in front of the mirrored wardrobe, Isabella impossibly elegant in jeans, leather boots and red cashmere, Cassie obsessively smoothing and tugging at the dark-green silk of her borrowed dress.

'You don't like it? You don't like my dress!'

'Isabella, I love your dress. It's what's inside it that looks like an idiot.'

'Tchah! You are blind as well as stupid.' Isabella tossed her hair. 'I'm looking *stunning*, darling, and you look twice as good as me. Of course, I'd like to think I am at least a little bit responsible for that.'

Cassie grinned. Things between her and Isabella had been surprisingly normal since the feeding tutorial, much to Cassie's relief. Even so, whatever Sir Alric said, she was planning to stretch things out as long as she possibly could before putting her friend – and herself – through the strange experience again.

She blinked at her reflection in the mirror. Her light-brown hair had had a proper cut – courtesy of Isabella again: how was she ever going to pay the girl back for this kindness as well as all the others? Now styled and smoothed, it had a satiny gleam. Isabella had chucked all Cassie's congealed and broken old lipsticks and eyeshadows into the bin, and worked some kind of magic with her own vastly expensive make-up kit. Staring into the mirror was like looking at a different person – a new, way-better-looking version of herself. She chuckled sardonically at her reflection and again pulled at her dress uncomfortably.

Isabella was right about one thing: she'd let herself get too thin – an invading spirit and the subsequent trauma would do that to a girl – but the colour of the fabric *did* bring out her eyes. The contrast with the rich, dark green made her yellow-green irises look brilliantly pale and piercing.

Her friend gave an exaggerated sigh. 'Trust me, you look fabulous, OK? Now get your Jimmy Choos on. You're going to party with your beau!'

'Get *your* Jimmy Choos on, you mean,' remarked Cassie under her breath, but she felt a thrill of glamour as she slipped into the gorgeous stilettos. 'Am I going to be able to walk?'

'In these shoes you do not walk, Cassie, you *stalk*.'

'Sure, whatever you say. I just wonder where I'm going dressed like this. I wish we were going to Coney Island with you guys.'

Perhaps she might even have had a chance to talk to Jake about his extra-curricular activities. Jake was still avoiding being alone with Cassie, and she was certain it was so that she couldn't pressure him to give up the hunt for Katerina.

'Don't be silly, your date will be *so* glamorous.' Isabella shook her head and sighed. 'Though mine is romantic, isn't it? Jake and I shall stroll on the boardwalk, arm in arm. We shall eat Nathan's hot dogs. We shall ride the Cyclone!'

'Uh-huh, so you have an excuse to scream and hang on to his neck.'

Isabella gave her a suggestive smile. 'What else is a rollercoaster for? Ah!' She gave a shriek of delight as a knock rattled the door of their room. 'Here he is!'

Here, as a matter of fact, were both of them, though they obviously hadn't planned to arrive together. Ranjit and Jake stood awkwardly, as far apart as they could reasonably be, their body language screaming their discomfort. As Isabella flung the door wide, their relief was palpable.

'Hey, gorgeous.' Jake's stiff expression melted into a huge grin as he swung Isabella in his arms. 'You look terrific!'

'Do not sound so surprised!' She kissed him with shameless enthusiasm. 'Shall we go and be tourists?'

'I am *dying* to be a tourist in my own city. Even if I can't take you somewhere expensive,' he muttered, with a slightly resentful glance at Ranjit's tuxedo.

'Hey! Just being with you is priceless!' Isabella punched his arm.

Meanwhile, Cassie found she couldn't meet Ranjit's eyes. She made herself clasp her fingers just to stop herself fiddling with her dress. Oh, God. What if she'd got this horribly wrong? What if he was embarrassed to be seen with her? What if . . .

His shoes were right there, though, so she had to look up and smile at him. That was when she knew it would be OK. His expression was one of startled awe, and there was even a hint of crimson in his dark cheekbones.

'Cassie.' He drew in a long breath, and shyly offered a yellow rose. 'You look . . . beautiful.'

'You too,' she blurted before she could stop herself. It was true, though. The tux must have been hand-made for him, perfectly fitted to his lithe body. She swore she could make out the lines of his muscles under the expensive fabric.

'Well, you guys.' Jake was clutching Isabella's hand, hesitating at the doorway and clearly desperate to leave. 'Have a good time.'

Ranjit cleared his throat. 'You too. Enjoy yourselves.'

Isabella was stifling laughter. 'Happy Valentine's Day,' she mouthed at Cassie. Then Jake was pulling her out of the room, the door swung shut, and they were gone.

Ranjit released a huge sigh of relief, and Cassie giggled.

'Cassandra Bell,' he grinned. 'Let's get out of here.'

It wasn't a long ride by yellow cab, but Ranjit insisted they couldn't walk – 'not in those fantastic shoes' – even though Cassie would have liked the fresh winter air. She only realised they had a deadline when the cab was pulling up on the corner of 57th Street and Seventh Avenue.

'Oh my God,' she breathed as she stepped out of the cab. 'I'm at Carnegie Hall.'

'How do you get to Carnegie Hall?' smiled Ranjit. 'Practise, practise . . .'

She giggled as she took his arm. 'That's a terrible joke.'

'That's a really *old* joke.' He glanced at his watch. 'We'd better take our seats. Come on.'

Cassie would have been happy sitting behind a pillar in the back row of the balcony, but they were guided to a box on the first tier, right at the front and overlooking the stage directly. It was such an exposed position she would have felt quite self-conscious, if it hadn't been for Ranjit's comforting hand in hers.

Then the curtain rose and she was instantly swept away by the music. Funny, she'd never heard anything by Richard Strauss in her life, and barely a note by Tchaikovsky or Beethoven, but straight away the music felt as if it belonged to her alone. Mesmerised, she was only vaguely aware of Ranjit's glances in her direction, but her senses sprang into overdrive when his fingertips stroked her hand. Crazily, tears pricked at her eyelids and she blinked them back. It would be stupid to cry, when she felt happier than she had in as long as she could remember.

Still, too many feelings were coming alive. She couldn't do anything to stop it, and she didn't want to. She was supremely aware of everything: the warmth of Ranjit's hand and the sharp tingle of her own nerves in response; the music, overwhelming her brain and her emotions, every single instrumental part sounding distinct in her head but every one harmonious with the next. She could taste the warmth and scent of the audience, breathing out and in, some of them occasionally holding their breath until the music made them release it in a rushing exhalation. She could hear the people as well as she could hear the music: the breathing, the rustle of silk and the occasional squeak of a leather shoe, the creak as someone shifted in a seat; the scrape of a bow across strings, the feathery whisper as a page of music was turned.

So it was inevitable that she'd feel a gaze if it was focused on her.

She was being watched. She knew it quite suddenly. Her forehead prickled with the stare, and for the first time she forgot the orchestra, forgot the soaring thunder of the music. When she lifted her own gaze, she knew the exact direction and she found the watcher immediately.

Shock hit her so hard she was left breathless. Across the auditorium, in the opposite box to their own, four girls sat. She knew them all: three sixth formers from the Academy, all Few. The superior Sara was one of them; Cassie didn't know the names of the two on either side of her, only that they'd never been friendly.

But the fourth face was one she knew all too well. Palely lovely, cold as the Arctic but glowing with beauty. An ice queen, a Hitchcock blonde. Perfect in every way – except for the scar slashed across her left cheek.

Cassie felt Ranjit's fingers tighten questioningly on her hand, but she was too frozen with shock to respond. Only when applause erupted to signify the interval did she snap out of it. The explosion of noise shattered her trance of horror and she turned to him with desperation.

'Katerina. Katerina's here!'

Ranjit frowned, but he didn't question her. He turned at her nod and stared in the direction of the opposite box. When Katerina lifted a delicate hand in a mocking little wave, he didn't react, but Cassie saw his eyes light with familiar fire. It was that swirling dark glow she'd seen before, like molten lava. It had been frightening the first time she'd seen it. This time it was strangely reassuring.

'I'm really sorry, Cassie.' Ranjit's voice was cool and deadly. 'I had no idea she was in New York.'

'It doesn't matter. Really.' Her heart was thrashing, at odds with her words. Katerina was in New York. Her mind flew to Jake. He had been hunting her all around the globe. What would he do if he found out she was here, in his home town? Within his reach . . . Ranjit's voice interrupted her thoughts.

'I had ordered champagne for the interval in the Members' Bar,' he said. 'But if you'd rather we stayed here . . .'

Cassie shook her head violently. 'I'm not about to let her spoil a lovely evening. We'll avoid them.'

He squeezed her hand. 'We'll certainly try. Come on.'

They should have been able to stay well out of the way

of Katerina and her friends, but despite the swelling crowds heading downstairs, Katerina was clearly determined not to stay out of theirs. Ranjit had just poured two frosty flutes of champagne in the Members' Bar when the blonde girl emerged from the smattering of well-heeled patrons, her friends flanking her like some kind of praetorian guard.

'Well, ding-dong Bell,' she drawled, giving Cassie a disdainful once-over. 'If it isn't the scholarship girl.'

'That's enough, Katerina.' Ranjit's voice was low and even, but there was a distinct undercurrent of threat to it.

'I quite agree. It's more than enough. For this lowlife to remain at the Academy while I was expelled is simply . . . Oh dear, how shall we put it?'

'A crime,' murmured Sara.

'That's kind, dear Sara, but crime can be fun and sophisticated.' Katerina gave a thin-lipped smile as the other three girls chuckled. 'There must be another word.'

'A disgrace,' suggested the brunette at Sara's side.

Cassie took a gulp of her champagne. The icy coolness hit her tongue and throat and rebounded straight to her head, but she didn't feel drunk: only cold and fierce. It felt good. Ranjit's arm was around her waist, at once protective and warning, but she didn't feel the need for his support. She took another swig from her glass, emptying it.

112

'Heavens, this isn't Sheffield town centre.' Sara's English accent was cut-crystal. 'We're not here to binge drink and vomit, Miss Bell.'

Katerina was still tapping her jaw gently with a finger. Cassie watched her face, fascinated by that scar. She remembered putting it there, back in that dark tunnel as she made her escape from the twisted Few ritual beneath the Arc de Triomphe. For the first time she was actively glad. Yes, that had been a good moment. In fact she'd like to do it again. Right now.

But Katerina was speaking again, distracting her.

'Hmm, I'm still trying to think of the appropriate term. Disgrace just doesn't begin to describe what happened last term. Sir Alric has plummeted in the estimation of many people. Such a decline in standards.'

'Leave here, Katerina.' Ranjit was absolutely still, but his voice was heavy with menace.

'Ah! I know the word,' said Sara, ignoring him. 'Let's see: a noble spirit inside something so unworthy. A mismatch. A freak. It should never have happened, Katerina darling, just like your expulsion. It's an . . . *abomination*.'

All four girls sighed out their satisfaction.

'Yes,' smirked Katerina. 'That's it precisely. An abomination.'

WHAT DID SHE CALL US?

The stem of Cassie's champagne flute snapped in her hand. She heard a strange growl, but it seemed to come from far away – or perhaps somewhere deep inside her. Her eyes burned hot, *so hot*, and everything had gone red, as though she was looking at the world through a scarlet filter. She registered the shock on Ranjit's face, and knew he was staring at her.

She could see the glow of the girls' spirits too, shining from their chests. They were all strong, particularly Katerina's, but she found she didn't care. Her own aura of power shrouded her, invisible but irresistible – and Cassie suddenly knew she could do anything she liked with this power, using nothing more than the force of her mind. She was entirely still. She didn't move a muscle.

And she lifted Sara's body clear into the air.

The girl took a breath and screamed. Her legs kicked the air, arms flailing in hopeless resistance, abject terror on her face.

Cassie enjoyed that. It was like feeding: the buzz, the thrill that went through her. She could almost taste Sara's fear in the air. It tasted good. So good.

She smiled, coldly fascinated, as drinkers around them backed away, silenced but for an occasional gasp or cry. Even Katerina and her cronies stood back, aghast.

'Cassie!' shouted Ranjit. Blood pumping through her

ears seemed to drown his voice out, along with Estelle's
fevered cries.

Kill her! KILL HER!

Yes. She was tired of the pathetic girl, trailing after
Katerina like some kind of handmaiden.

She called us an abomination!

Kill her!

Yes! Kill her!

'Cassie, no!'

People in the bar stumbled away, frantically forcing their
way out of the secluded Members' area. Cassie ignored
them, laughing as she watched Sara flail. The girl's face!
Ridiculous! She laughed again and, still without lifting a
finger, flung the screaming sixth former across the room.

The girl shot backwards, slamming hard against the far
wall. Katerina howled with rage, and the other girls
screamed – but they seemed rooted to the spot, unwilling
to challenge Cassie. Afraid of her.

As well they should be. We should have thrown her further!
Hold her!

Cassie studied Sara. It was a fine sight, the girl
struggling to get to her feet. Yes, Estelle was right. Hold
her. She must hold her. Just like this. By the throat.

'Cassie, stop!'

The dear boy. But such an irritant! Don't listen.

Shaking her head free of Ranjit's cries, she tightened her mental hold on Sara's neck, squeezing. The girl was purpling, fighting for another breath, kicking violently, tearing at her own throat and the invisible grip around it. Odd noises came out of her. Gagging, choking, strangled sounds.

'CASSIE!'

She felt arms lock around her waist, and suddenly someone was struggling with her, trying to pull her away. She took a breath to give a contemptuous laugh, and raised an arm to brush them away. But the hand that seized hers was just as strong as hers.

Ranjit!

The shock of his touch brought her back to herself, and she realised where she was. *Who* she was.

What she was doing.

'STOP IT!' Ranjit's snarl was inhuman, catlike, but she understood it clearly.

Besides, she'd already stopped. In the silence of the emptied Members' Bar, watched only by monsters like herself, Cassie stared at Sara's limp form as it crumpled, sobbing, to the floor.

CHAPTER ELEVEN

Oh yes, you could run in Jimmy Choos. Really, *really* fast. Cassie shoved through the crowds in the foyer, the bewildered ones who hadn't been in the bar to see what had happened. Outside, the cold air hit her like a slap as she bolted across 57th Street and Central Park South, into the dark safety of the park itself.

She went on running until the high heels began to – not hurt her, but annoy her. Anger again. No. She mustn't get angry. Stumbling to a halt, she tugged off the shoes and ran on barefoot, her breathing hard and ragged, the straps of the stilettos hooked into her fingers.

Something soft and cold touched the skin of her face. And once more. Halting, she stood uncertainly for a few seconds. The coldness turned to wetness as it brushed her cheek.

Snow. The flakes drifted faster and thicker across the

city's lights before vanishing in the dark oasis of the park. Her bare feet were freezing. *She* was freezing. She could see only scattered pools of light on whitening patches of grass, and the ominous shape of trees. She wrapped her arms around herself, shaking with terror. *Oh, God!*

A dark shape moved behind her, and she gave a sharp cry of fear.

'Cassie.'

His voice was quiet, and the animal ferocity was gone. She turned into Ranjit's arms with a desperate sob of relief.

'Come on, Cassie. Let's go.'

'I don't know what this is. I've never heard of it.'

Sir Alric Darke's back was turned to them. For several silent minutes now he had been staring out of the glass walls of his penthouse on to the glittering lights of Manhattan and the blackness that was Central Park.

Cassie shivered. She could hardly believe she'd run into that absorbing darkness without a thought. The hunger was growing again; she could feel it. It had gnawed at her insides since she'd run in a blind panic from Carnegie Hall. The spirit was awake and it was ravenous. And that was one more thing she didn't need, because she'd been just as sure as Ranjit that Sir Alric could explain what had happened at Carnegie Hall.

No such luck.

'You say you picked Sara up?'

'Not – not physically.' Her voice trembled, and she cleared her throat. 'But yes, I picked her up. Some kind of force. Outside me, but it felt like I was controlling it.'

'This is baffling. And it worries me a great deal.'

'It worries *you*?' She tried to laugh.

'Sir Alric,' Ranjit broke in. 'If you can't explain what's happened, no one can. There must be something. Something you've forgotten, something from the past.'

'I'm touched by your faith in me, Ranjit.' Sir Alric sounded unusually bitter. 'But no. I've never heard of any such thing. I'd remember, believe me.'

Ranjit squeezed Cassie's shoulders in an attempt to reassure her. 'Are you sure that the joining ritual has never been broken before?'

Sir Alric gazed out on the city again. 'No. No, Ranjit, it hasn't. And you're right, it's the only thing that's different about Cassie: her interrupted ritual.'

'Some of the spirit was shut out,' said Cassie quietly. 'Some of Estelle. She talks about being out in a void.'

Sir Alric spun sharply on his heel. 'She talks to you? You *hear* her voice?'

'Yes.' Cassie's shoulders sagged.

'That shouldn't happen,' he muttered, rubbing his forehead. 'That shouldn't happen.'

'She wants to be *let in*. Like you told me at the end of last term. You said she wouldn't stop until she joined with me fully.'

Sir Alric stayed silent but nodded slowly, his brows knitted.

'What's happening to me?' Cassie's voice took on an air of desperation.

Sir Alric's eyes met hers. 'I don't know.'

Gently easing from Ranjit's hold, Cassie rose to her feet. 'You're hardly filling me with confidence here.'

'I'm sorry. There are some people I can ask and some ancient texts I can consult, but for now, Cassandra, I can't give you any firm answers.'

'Oh, brilliant.' She folded her arms.

'Part of the spirit you think of as Estelle was shut out of you. She's divided, so perhaps your power is divided, too.' He shook his head despairingly. 'It's the only explanation I have, Cassandra. When we join with our spirits, the power that they provide goes *inside* us, becomes part of us. But your spirit is not fully joined with your body, so perhaps you can project some of your power beyond yourself. I'm not sure.'

Resting a shoulder against the glass, Cassie too gazed

out at the sparkling grid of the city streets. Then she straightened, brightening suddenly.

'Then . . . hang on a minute. If part of the power is outside, maybe I can get it all out?' She turned to face Sir Alric, excited. 'Get rid of it and get rid of Estelle!'

Deep inside her she thought she heard a whimper of fear, a whine of protest, but she ignored it.

Ranjit stood up now, his jaw tense. 'Is that what you want, Cassie? Truly?'

'Of course! Wouldn't you?'

He didn't answer, only held her gaze. For a moment they regarded one another silently.

'Cassandra,' said Sir Alric finally breaking the silence. 'You have to be extremely careful. We don't know what you're capable of. Whatever this power is, it appears to be very dangerous. What's more, your spirit absolutely will not want to leave you. Without your body, it will be lost in the void for ever. Believe me, it will hold on to you at all costs. Who knows what Estelle might do if she believes she's threatened? Until we know more about your power, you absolutely must not provoke her.'

'And how exactly do I avoid provoking her?' Cassie glared at them both. 'She's got a mind of her own, let me tell you.'

'You can start by controlling your emotions,' Sir Alric

snapped sharply. 'It was your fury that sparked the spirit's power tonight. Do not let that happen again.'

'Oh, sure, no worries,' she growled sarcastically. 'Piece of piss.'

Ranjit gave an exasperated sigh. 'Cassie, he's trying to help.'

She whirled to face him. 'Don't patronise me! "Control my emotions"? Well, guess what, that's far bloody easier said than done. I didn't ask for this, so just how the hell do you expect me to know how to control it?'

'You must try, Cassandra,' Sir Alric said wearily.

'Come on, Cassie,' Ranjit said gently. He reached over to take her hand, and she reluctantly allowed him. 'There's nothing more we can do tonight. Let's leave it for now. See what Sir Alric can find out.' He nodded towards the principal. 'Goodnight.'

Cassie noticed a shadow cross Sir Alric's expression as he watched Ranjit put an arm around her and lead her out.

'Goodnight.'

The door closed silently behind them. Cassie was all too happy to leave the penthouse office. Ranjit, though, was silent and withdrawn. Hardly surprising, she decided. He'd taken her straight to Sir Alric, certain that he would provide both an explanation and assistance.

And look how it had turned out. Sir Alric Darke was no more use to them than Sara's feeble Few powers had been to her . . .

'Are you sure Sara was all right?' she ventured, reddening as she remembered the reason for her flight from Carnegie Hall.

Ranjit shrugged. 'Well, she was alive.'

Cassie sighed deeply. 'I wish none of this had ever happened.'

'Too late, Cassie.' He was quiet for a long moment, but then spoke again, a glint playing darkly in his eyes. 'But you know what? Whatever the reason for it, the truth is you were magnificent tonight. So strong. I . . . I couldn't take my eyes off you.'

Cassie stayed silent for a moment, unsure what such an admission might mean, or how to reply. She settled on the truth.

'Whatever the reason . . . I enjoyed doing it.' She paused. 'Doesn't that scare you? I know it scares me.'

'Yes, it does. But I can't deny my nature.' He shook his head. 'Let's not talk about that right now. You've been through a lot tonight. You should get some sleep.'

'But I – I thought we could hang out a bit.' Cassie found she was desperate to keep him with her, to have presence for a little longer. 'I'm not tired . . .'

'*I am.*' But he reached out to her all the same, pulling her closer, almost as if he didn't know he was doing it. 'Surely you must be too.'

'I'm not,' Cassie murmured. Her eyes swept urgently around his face, her hands moving up to caress it, unthinkingly. He seemed bewildered, his breathing heavy.

She drew in a breath to say something else. Too late. His mouth was suddenly on hers, his tongue finding her tongue and striking sparks off her nerve endings. For an instant the tide of lust held her immobilised; then she was returning the kiss, passionately, almost violently. Her arms snaked round his neck, warm under her touch, and she drew him closer, so close, as if their bodies were trying to fuse together.

Yesss . . .

Estelle's voice inside her mind, echoing her thoughts once more.

Together, we must be, all of us . . . !

Suddenly, Cassie felt Ranjit's fingers in her hair, tugging it, pulling it taut. She gave a gasp of pain but then drew his mouth to hers once more. She sucked his lower lip between her teeth, biting down hard, almost drawing blood – there was an urgency, a violence developing between them, but she felt powerless to break their embrace . . .

'STOP THIS AT ONCE!'

The barked order was sudden and fierce. Ranjit's head snapped back, breaking contact. Cassie growled in frustration. It took her a moment to realise that Sir Alric stood beside them, framed in the doorway of his office, his shoulders tense and his hands clenched into fists.

Ranjit seemed stunned into silence for a beat, licking a drop of blood from his lips. 'I'm sorry—'

Don't apologise, lover . . .

'Don't apologise,' Cassie heard herself echo, and the words brought her back to cold reality. Had Ranjit been apologising to her, or to Sir Alric?

'I think both of you should proceed to your own rooms forthwith,' said Sir Alric through gritted teeth.

Ranjit nodded, looking shaken. Cassie frowned. What was his problem? Of course it was a bit embarrassing to be caught kissing by the principal, but they weren't really doing anything really wrong, were they?

Ranjit stepped away from her, very deliberately. She shook her head, and gave a mirthless laugh.

'Night, Ranjit.'

'Goodnight, Cassie.' His eyes still held a shade of longing.

Frustrated, she turned away without a second glance at

Sir Alric. But as she walked down the hall she heard the principal's voice, low and severe.

'A word before you go, Mr Singh.'

Cassie turned, confused, and saw Ranjit give her a brief last glance before disappearing back into the office. What was that about?

Next time, my dear, we must try harder. This simply will not do . . .

CHAPTER TWELVE

'Jake? What are you doing here?'

Cassie had been trying to turn the door handle quietly so as not to wake her roommate, when the door suddenly swung open, making her jump. Why would Jake be leaving her and Isabella's room so late in the evening? Then she remembered the couple's date, and couldn't help allowing a little smile to cross her lips. 'Oops. Hope I haven't interrupted anything?'

Jake's face was serious. 'Uh, Cassie, can I talk to you for a sec?'

Her heart skipped a beat. He'd been avoiding her for weeks, why did he want to talk to her now? Had he found out about the feeding? No, he wouldn't even be speaking to her if that were the case. Did he know what had happened earlier with Katerina? She wasn't expecting to have to deal with that aspect of the evening's events quite so soon . . .

Jake stepped outside and pulled the door shut quietly. 'I'm glad you're back. Isabella's gonna need someone with her tonight.'

'What's wrong?'

'We just had a bit of a scare at Coney Island is all. It's OK. She'll be fine once she's had a chance to rest.'

Cassie's brow furrowed. 'What happened?'

'Maybe it's nothing.' He seemed to hesitate for a moment, and then muttered, 'I think we're all just a little tense, maybe imagining things.'

'What are you talking about?'

Jake forced a smile. 'Look, just do your girl thing, look out for her, and I'll catch up with you guys when I can tomorrow.'

'I thought we were all going to hook up in the morning and go to Chinatown? You know, Isabella's whole plan to hang out and do normal things?' She smiled, but Jake's face was serious again.

'Not in the morning. I have a few things I need to take care of.' He leaned over and kissed Cassie briskly on the cheek. 'Night.'

Cassie stared after him, bemused. This was definitely one of the strangest nights she'd ever had. She turned away and inched the door open.

'Cassie?' Isabella sat up in bed.

'Yeah, it's me. Busted. I was trying to be quiet . . .'

'It's OK. I was awake.'

Cassie peered at her friend in the dimness as she closed the door. Isabella was hugging her knees, staring not at Cassie but at the wall. 'Hey, what's going on? Jake said something happened on your date.'

'Uh . . .' For once Isabella seemed to be lost for words. 'It . . . ah . . . didn't go quite to plan.'

Isabella was trembling, Cassie noticed. Sitting down beside her, she put an arm round her. She felt cold. A sense of dread rose in her.

'Isabella, what happened? Did you guys have a row or—'

'No! No, nothing like that.' Isabella shook her head violently. 'It went really well, to start with. We were having a great time. Then – oh, it was horrible, Cassie. I know this is going to sound crazy . . .' She trailed off, and Cassie's eyes widened with worry at Isabella's glum features.

'What is it, Isabella?'

Isabella rubbed her goose-pimpled arms. 'It's just . . . well, I think someone tried to abduct me.'

'What? Isabella! What the hell happened?'

Isabella exhaled. 'We were at the back of the line for the

rollercoaster. There was a really long wait, and so Jake had offered to go and get me some cotton candy while I kept our place. After a few moments, I felt a hand reach around from behind and grab me . . .' She looked up at Cassie, her voice dropping to a whisper. 'I thought it was Jake being playful, but then they were dragging me away, and there was a hand over my mouth. I couldn't scream . . . It was only because Jake came and saw. He shouted – oh Cassie, you should have heard him! You would have thought he had seen a ghost he looked so frightened. Then a security guard came, and whoever it was dropped me and ran before they could catch up . . .'

'Isabella, that's *awful*!'

'If Jake hadn't seen what was happening . . . If he hadn't shown up when he did, I don't know what would have happened.' Isabella shivered, hugging her legs tighter.

'You're safe now.' Cassie squeezed her shoulders comfortingly. She shook her head. 'Why on earth would someone do that?'

Isabella shook her head. 'I don't know. Maybe they wanted my handbag? Jake said he thought he saw someone watching us when we were riding the carousel, but I thought he was just being paranoid. But now . . . Oh Cassie, I don't want to think about it any more.'

'Of course not. Look, you should try and get some rest.'

'I'll be all right, Cassie.' Isabella paused, huddling under her bedclothes, then smiled again weakly. 'But I am a terrible friend – I haven't even asked about *your* date! Was it fabulous?'

'Well.' Cassie gave a short laugh. 'Ours was kind of eventful too . . .'

'Wow.' Isabella made a show of resetting her dropped jaw as Cassie finished relating the story of Carnegie Hall, the strange powers she had exhibited, and Sir Alric's inability to explain what had happened. She left out the part about him catching her and Ranjit kissing. Something about the intensity of their clinch made her uncomfortable talking about it. And she has to ask Isabella not to tell Jake about Katerina.

'Cassie, I don't know what to say. That's some date. But I'm sure Sir Alric is going to figure out what happened.'

Cassie studied her friend for a moment. There was a faint glimmer of trepidation in Isabella's eyes, but that was understandable given what Cassie had just described. She shook her head, trying not to think too hard about it all. 'Yeah. Up until all that happened, it was amazing. Mind you, I was thinking I'd have swapped the whole experience for a Coney Island hot dog, but now I'm not so sure.'

'Funny how things went wrong for both of us, isn't it?'

'Mmm. Hilarious.' Cassie grimaced.

Isabella gave a great sigh. 'Cassie. Let's forget it for tonight. It's as you said. We both need some sleep.'

RANJIT!

Cassie was running again. Running towards him, everything was bathed in that nightmarish red glow, and . . .

RANJIT!

Catch him, hold him . . .

I WILL, ESTELLE! THIS TIME WE WON'T FAIL . . .

'Cassie? Cassie!' Isabella's face loomed into view, her expression a mixture of amusement and concern. 'Hey, Cassie? Wakey-wakey, as you say!'

Blearily, Cassie pulled down the covers and blinked at her roommate. 'What's the time?'

'Time to get up. Come on. All night you were tossing and turning, but this morning – you sleep like a stick! I thought I was bad . . .'

'Sleep like a log, Isabella. Like a log.'

Cassie sat up, her face hot remembering her dream. At least Isabella seemed to have cheered up after last night. She was amazed at the girl's ability to compartmentalise –

she'd trade that skill for the invisible force thing anytime.

'Come on,' Isabella chirped. 'We need a change of scene. Particularly as I bet you anything you're the hot topic around these parts this morning.'

'What?' Cassie rubbed her eyes. 'Oh God, yes. Carnegie Hall.'

Isabella was right – Sara would have come running back to tell the rest of the Few about the freakish powers of their newest member. Cassie groaned.

'Let's get out of everyone's way,' suggested Isabella. 'We'll head to Chinatown early, have breakfast?'

'Sounds like a good idea to me,' agreed Cassie, swinging herself out of bed. She was barely awake, but already she could feel the hunger for life-energy gnawing at her. Sir Alric's instructions about regular feeding came back to her, but she brushed them aside. She wasn't ready to try feeding again. Maybe some normal food would help take her mind off it.

'Great,' beamed Isabella. 'I'll call Jake and let him know.'

'Uh, Isabella.' Cassie turned to her roommate. 'Jake said he can't make it this morning. Didn't he tell you last night?'

Isabella looked confused. 'Can't make it? Why not?'

'I . . . He didn't exactly say,' admitted Cassie reluctantly.

'He said he'd meet us later.'

Come to think of it, that was a pretty poor show. What could be more important than comforting your girlfriend the day after someone had tried to abduct her?

Isabella seemed to be wondering that too, judging by the hurt expression on her pretty features. Then she rallied, briskly pulling on clothes, and as usual turning out carelessly elegant even though she barely seemed to check what she hauled from the wardrobe.

'Well, at least that means after we eat, we could go and hit some shops, no?'

'Mmm, I'll definitely need to line my stomach then!' Cassie hopped awkwardly into her jeans, then rummaged frantically in a drawer for a sweater.

Isabella had moved on to her make-up before Cassie had even brushed her teeth. She was humming to herself and comparing two lipsticks as Cassie observed her from the en suite bathroom sink. Must have decided to put the Coney Island accident right out of her mind, she thought. That was probably for the best. Swiftly, she exited the bathroom, quickly running a brush through her hair.

'Nearly there. You ready?'

'Uh-huh. Now, where did I put my bangle?' Isabella swept her hand through the chaos on her nightstand, then stopped. 'Oh no!'

Her cry of horror got Cassie's attention straight away. 'What?'

Wordlessly, Isabella lifted the bangle on one finger. It was one of her favourites: chunky and fun, like a very beautiful piece of costume jewellery, but made out of solid 24-carat gold.

And it had melted.

Cassie stared at it, dangling on Isabella's finger. Her friend's face was stricken, but she couldn't get out a word of sympathy. Her throat seemed to have seized up altogether.

'How did this happen?' wailed Isabella, trying to force the warped gold on to her slender wrist. 'I must have left it too close to the radiator.'

Or maybe too close to me, thought Cassie dully. Isabella's nightstand was between her bed and Cassie's. And the melted-wax look of the metal was hideously familiar . . .

'Ugh! Oh well. Never mind.' Isabella tossed the ruined bangle on to the bed and forced her face into a smile. 'I won't let it spoil our day. Come on!'

I'll probably take care of that, Cassie thought as they gathered their coats and bags and scarves and headed out. What the hell was going on? How could she be melting solid gold bangles and silver photo frames in her sleep?

She remembered Sir Alric's words: *Perhaps you can project some of your power beyond yourself.*

Well, if this was something to do with her power, then that power seemed to making its presence felt more and more strongly. Was it reaching out to those close to her? Oh, God . . .

If she could destroy solid metal, what could she do to flesh and bone?

What could she do to her friends?

CHAPTER THIRTEEN

'Well, this certainly is a change of scene.'

Dodging a fish seller, Isabella tucked her arm cheerfully through Cassie's. 'Just what we both need.'

That was for sure. Cassie was glad to get away from Fifth Avenue and Central Park – all the Upper East Side environs of the Academy – so it was fun to squeeze into a tiny old Chatham Square teahouse for breakfast. Afterwards, they strolled through Columbus Park and meandered aimlessly through the bustling vendors and tourists on Mulberry and Canal Streets. In crowded lanes and shop fronts, decorations from Chinese New Year still lingered, tatty but cheerful. In spite of herself, Cassie felt her mood lift.

It was noisy, rowdy and chaotic; between the shouts of vendors, the blare and roar of cars and the music spilling from restaurants, Cassie could barely hear herself think.

More to the point, she couldn't hear Estelle think. And despite the growing hunger inside her, the drifting scents of temple incense and cooking food made it all but impossible to smell human breath, even for her heightened senses.

How Isabella heard her phone she couldn't imagine, but the girl stopped suddenly and answered it. Cassie could hear nothing of the conversation, but from her roommate's doe-eyes, it didn't take a rocket scientist to guess who was calling.

'Cassieeee,' wheedled Isabella, flipping her phone shut and sidestepping a vendor selling ripped-off DVDs. 'That was Jake! Is it OK if we meet up after all?'

Cassie came to a halt by a stand piled with leaf-wrapped packets of rice. 'Uh, of course. Why wouldn't it be?'

'Well, you know . . .' Isabella shook her head at the rice seller and they moved along. 'I *have* noticed that it's been a bit awkward between you and him these past weeks, no?'

Cassie cursed silently. Not Isabella as well. Why did she have to have such astute friends . . .

'Well, we are keeping a pretty big secret from him, Isabella,' Cassie replied disingenuously. 'I feel bad about it.'

She couldn't bring herself to explain the real reason for the tension. Isabella would freak out big time if she knew Jake was hunting for Katerina.

'So do I, but it's for the best, Cassie. You mustn't tell! Swear it. You mustn't. If you think that being part of the Few is affecting your friendship with him now, imagine if he knows about the feeding!'

Cassie shuddered. She could imagine all too well. 'Yeah. I know.'

'Things will work out. He adores you, Cassie. It's just that he's got issues, you know that. About Ranjit. And Jessica. And . . .'

Cassie gave an exasperated moan, raking her fingers through her hair. 'Look, I can't blame Jake for being loyal to his sister. But if he'd just try to get to know Ranjit a little he'd be able to see that he would never have deliberately led Jess into the trap. I can understand that us being together is hard for him . . .' She tailed off. 'It's kind of hard for me too,' she said, mostly to herself.

Isabella patted her arm. 'Well, Jake and Ranjit will come around to each other eventually. They have to – we need to be able to double date!' She smiled, then gave a loud dramatic sigh, flinging out her arms so violently she almost knocked a wrinkled old lady off her bike. 'But if you would rather not see Jake right now, I can call it off . . .'

'Don't be crazy, Isabella. Of course we'll meet up with Jake!'

Isabella grinned. 'I knew you'd say that.'

'Oh did you now! Drama queen. Don't wave your arms again, you nearly killed someone. Where are we meeting?'

'Outside the Lincoln Center, on the West Side. One o'clock.' Isabella checked her watch, and walked faster, calling back happily to her friend. 'We'll have lunch, do some retail therapy . . . It'll be like old times, Cassie!'

'You can think about lunch already? You amaze me.' Swallowing her misgivings, Cassie laughed. 'Come on, then. And don't you dare call another cab. We'll take the subway.'

Isabella was racing ahead of Cassie with every step – she must have been dying to meet up with Jake. The Argentinean girl was as happy as . . . as a polo pony in fresh hay, or something. It was quite reassuring to see that it was possible to be so into someone despite all the craziness around them. It gave Cassie hope for her and Ranjit.

All the same, when they reached the Lincoln Center plaza and caught sight of Jake sitting on the edge of the fountain – tapping at his laptop, *again* – Cassie couldn't help hanging back. She wasn't sure how long she could conceal the fact that Katerina, his sister's killer, was swanning around this very city. Jake, though, jumped up straight away, shoving his laptop swiftly into its case and jogging over. As soon as he could bring himself to let go of Isabella, he gave Cassie a quick hug too, though there was some tension in his eyes she couldn't quite read – as though he was hiding something, holding something back . . . Isabella seemed oblivious.

'Now, where shall we eat? Oh, it's so good to be together again!'

Yes, thought Cassie, even though there was one vital person absent. Seeing Isabella link her fingers through Jake's made her realise just how much she was missing Ranjit, despite having seen him only last night.

Last night.

She felt a knot in her stomach at the ambiguous way they had left things, Sir Alric's interruption and . . . what had come before that. She couldn't figure out what it was between them – the magnetic push and pull of it was tough to get her head around. He liked her, didn't he? He must do, to risk the disdain of so many of the Few. And the spark between them – it was like something out of this world. There was no reason to be afraid, was there?

'No way am I trailing you round Bloomingdale's all afternoon while you try on half the store,' Jake was telling Isabella, though he looked to Cassie as if he'd trail her to the ends of the earth if she crooked one little finger.

'Oh, it's only a little shopping. Don't be such a spoilsport. Oh! We had breakfast, Jake! We puffed our faces at a wonderful teahouse. All red banquettes and—'

'Cool. I'm glad you had a chilled out morning, after everything that happened last night.'

'So if shopping's off the agenda, what do you reckon we should do instead, Jake?' Cassie said, eyeing him closely. He seemed to brighten.

'Uh, I dunno . . . Some sightseeing? How about the Chrysler Building, or Times Square? Or St Patrick's! Like I said, it's fun being a tourist in my own place. I never saw it like this before.'

'I still want to see *some* shops!' Isabella punched Jake affectionately in the solar plexus, making him almost double up. 'Oh, in fact – look at these . . .' She sped off towards an expensive-looking shop window and began gazing at the display of handbags, her eyes wide with excitement. Cassie stepped towards her half-heartedly, but stopped when Jake whispered her name urgently.

'Cassie . . .'

She turned, glancing at Isabella, then walked over to him, her nerves tumbling in her stomach. Whatever it was he wanted to talk about, it wasn't going to be good. She stopped beside him and he fixed her with a serious gaze.

'What?'

'Listen, I know this is going to sound crazy, but I think we could all be in danger.'

Cassie's eyes widened. 'Danger? What do you mean?'

'Last night . . . The person who tried to grab Isabella . . .' Jake drew a deep breath and ran his hand over his short hair. 'I think it was Katerina.'

'*What?* No, Jake—'

'Look, I know what you're going to say – that I'm so obsessed that I'm seeing things – but I got a good look, and I swear to God it was her.'

'Jake, it wasn't her.' Cassie grabbed his arm as he tried to interrupt. 'Listen to me. I *know* it wasn't her. Katerina can't have been at Coney Island with you and Isabella last night.'

'How can you be so sure?' he demanded angrily.

'Because she was at Carnegie Hall. I saw her.'

That shut him up. In fact, for a moment she thought it had given him a stroke. Jake's eyes bulged disbelievingly as he tried to absorb her words. Finally, he spoke.

'Why didn't you tell me last night?' he demanded.

'You didn't give me a chance, remember?' she snapped. 'You had *things to take care of* – things that didn't include your girlfriend, obviously.'

Jake bridled. 'Yeah, I had to get back to Coney Island

in case Katerina was still there. Which I wouldn't have had to do if you'd bothered to mention that you'd seen her on the other side of New York.'

Cassie winced inwardly. Why couldn't she keep her temper? Jake glanced in Isabella's direction as she called over.

'I'm just going inside for a sec, guys . . .'

He waved, and turned back to Cassie.

'Look, I was going to tell you about Katerina,' she said, getting her words in first. 'I just needed to find the right time.'

'So what happened? At Carnegie Hall? Did you talk to her?'

Cassie grimaced. 'Sort of. But trust me – it was her.'

Jake chewed his lip anxiously. 'I would have bet my life it was Katerina at Coney Island, but I guess I must have been imagining things. Unless the Few can be in two places at once.'

Despite herself, Cassie laughed. 'I don't think so.'

Jake shook his head. 'But then on the subway today, I was sure I was being followed again. Something's up, Cassie. You and I, we're in this deep – me with Jess, and you with your . . . ritual. But Isabella doesn't have to be involved.'

Cassie's stomach lurched horribly. If only he knew . . .

Jake didn't seem to notice. 'Promise me you won't tell Isabella.'

'Jake, I can't do that.'

'I have to make sure that Katerina can't do it again, Cassie. I have to find her. I've gotta go.'

'Go where?'

Cassie jumped as Isabella popped up at her side, shifting a huge shopping bag from one hand to the other. Jake twisted his face into an exasperated grin and held his hands up apologetically.

'Back to the Academy. I just had a phone call,' Jake lied. 'Chelnikov wants to see me. I kinda failed to hand in a couple of essays. I guess I've just been a bit preoccupied.'

'Your tutor wants to see you on a Saturday? Jake, that's not fair!'

'I know, but he insists. I have to go *now*. He means business, Isabella, I can't say no. I'm in enough trouble with that guy already.'

'He's got no right.' Isabella was pouting furiously.

'He's got my school career in his hands,' pointed out Jake. 'I gotta go. I'm really sorry, babe.' He tried to smile, though he wouldn't look Cassie in the eye. 'You'll have a great time without me. Go on, spend your socks off.'

'Sure.' Isabella tilted her chin reluctantly to receive his kiss. 'See you, Jake.'

Cassie's brow creased, and she didn't reply when he said goodbye to her. There were far too many lies floating about – something would have to give eventually. Now on top of everything else she had to worry about Jake stepping up his pursuit of Katerina, now he knew she was in the city . . .

'Chelnikov!' Isabella pouted. 'Why does that . . . that *drill sergeant* need to see him on a weekend!'

'I don't know, but Jake wouldn't go unless he really had to, would he?' Cassie cringed, kicking herself for covering for him. She just didn't want to give Isabella another reason to worry.

Isabella shrugged resignedly and ran her hands through her mane of hair. 'OK, you're right. It's not his fault. Oh, why was I so mean to him?'

'Beats me,' Cassie said reluctantly.

Isabella linked her arm through her friend's once more. 'Well, I will make it up to him later,' she said archly. 'In the meantime, a trip around Bloomingdale's should raise my spirits.'

Maybe, thought Cassie darkly. Let's hope it doesn't raise mine . . .

CHAPTER FOURTEEN

'That was fun!' said Cassie.

She actually almost meant it – Isabella's enthusiasm for shopping was infectious, and helped take Cassie's mind off things, for a moment at least. 'I take it you're suitably consoled?'

'Ooof!' came Isabella's reply. She halted in the Academy's atrium, right next to Achilles, and set down her collection of shopping bags. Cassie sighed as well, all too aware of the stares and whispers of the Few that followed her. The Carnegie Hall story had obviously gone round the common room like wildfire. Mikhail in particular gave her a filthy glare as he passed. If some of the Few had been unwelcoming before, she dreaded to think how they'd feel towards her now.

Stretching her shoulders, Isabella bent and tweaked open one bag. Achilles' blank eyes glowered straight into it.

'He doesn't approve,' remarked Cassie, jerking her thumb at the young marble warrior.

'That tells me all I need to know,' sniffed Isabella. 'He is a man with no heart. Look at the way he treats poor Hector.' Affectionately she patted Hector's cold marble arm, raised in futile protest at his imminent death. 'Yes. I consider myself consoled. Bergdorf Goodman was a particular triumph.'

'Girls, you have been *very* naughty.'

For a fleeting second Cassie imagined it was Achilles talking, till she saw Richard. He was propped lazily against the statue, one hand on Achilles' toned butt. A group of Few girls stared at him, then over towards Cassie, clearly disbelieving and hostile. Richard seemed to ignore them.

'Richard!' Isabella kissed him on both cheeks, before shooting a guilty look at Cassie. 'That's the pot calling the skittle black, I think. Weren't you at Gucci yesterday when you should have been in French literature?'

Richard grinned slyly. '*Touché!* Fabulous coat, bella Isabella. Cassie, you're looking stunning, as ever.'

She gave him a tight smile through gritted teeth, but remained stonily silent. It was all she could do not to throttle him. Isabella's presence was pretty much all that was stopping her. So what if he came over all penitent and guilty? She didn't trust him as far as she could throw— She cut herself off mid-thought. After the events of last night, that wasn't such a comfortable metaphor.

Richard unwound a cashmere scarf from his neck, and lowered his voice. 'Cassie, darling, you have to forgive me eventually.'

'I don't think so,' Cassie snapped.

'Well.' He raised a hand at a tall, shy-looking, new sixth-form girl, who blushed and smiled as she swept her overlong blonde fringe out of her eyes. 'I fear I must take my leave.'

'Oh, Richard,' scolded Isabella, following his eye-line. 'You're impossible.'

'On the contrary, I'm all too probable. And, oh dear, here comes Daniel again,' sighed Richard as he caught sight of a well-built Israeli boy making a beeline towards them. 'I have a stalker, ladies. One little dalliance and now he won't leave me alone. Once you go *fop*, it appears you can't stop . . . Farewell.' With a last flirtatious wink at the blonde sixth former, Richard dodged swiftly out of sight towards the elevators, leaving Daniel to glare hatred.

'He'll never change,' said Isabella, shaking her head. She looked cautiously over at Cassie. 'Do you think you could *ever* forgive him?'

'No.'

When they reached the elevator, it felt like a haven from the whispers and the watchers. Cassie pressed the button with a sigh of relief. 'I wonder if Ranjit's around.'

'If Ranjit's around, I'm sure he'll find you,' teased Isabella, lugging her retail haul into their room and dumping the bags on her bed. 'Hey, what's that?'

'Good question.' Cassie dropped her own rather smaller shopping bag on the floor, eyeing the scroll that lay on her pillow. It was gilt-edged – that was new – but it was tied in a familiar black ribbon. A shiver of fear travelled up her spine. Nothing good ever seemed to come of these sinister messages. Why couldn't the Academy use email like everyone else?

'Go on, open it!'

Reluctant even to touch the scroll, Cassie cautiously broke the wax seal on the ribbon. Unrolling it with the tip of a fingernail, she read the message through in silence.

Isabella had entirely forgotten Bergdorf Goodman. She was watching Cassie with unbearable curiosity. 'Come on! Give!'

Cassie frowned. 'It's from the Council of Elders. Whatever that is.'

'Sounds good.' Isabella hesitated, then glanced doubtfully at Cassie. 'Doesn't it?'

'No. It's a summons to a meeting of the Council

next week. Attendance is not optional.'

Angrily, Cassie flung the scroll to the floor, and Isabella lifted it gingerly to read it through herself. She raised her eyebrows. 'It's rather curt, isn't it?'

'Yeah, well I think I can guess what it's about.'

The girls looked at each other, and neither was smiling. They said the words in unison.

'Carnegie Hall.'

'Cassie, hi!'

Ranjit's face lit up as he raised his head from the pile of books at his desk. It hadn't been difficult to find him: huddled in a quiet nook of the vast library, poring over ancient books that seemed very out of place among the sleek hyper-modern facilities. His expression darkened again as he read her own. 'What's up?'

Cassie wanted to fling the scroll down – she hated even touching it – but she managed to lay the rolled-up parchment carefully in front of him, on top of his open book.

His eyes widened. 'The Council of Elders.'

'You've had one of these?' She raised her eyebrows quizzically.

Ranjit shook his head. 'No. But I recognise the style.' He fingered the scroll's gilt edging thoughtfully.

'It arrived today. While I was out, of course.'

'I see.' He sat back in his chair, turning a pen in his fingers, then looked up at her, his eyes searching. 'How are you, Cassie? I'm sorry I didn't get to walk you to your room last night . . . And for how things turned out in general. I'll make it up to you, I promise.' He laughed briefly and gave her an apologetic look. 'I seem to be finding myself saying that to you a lot.'

Cassie smiled. 'I'm OK. I think I may be starting to get a little, uh, hungry, but it's nothing I can't handle.' Noticing his concerned look, she pressed on, hoping to distract him. 'So, what did Sir Alric say to you last night anyway? Birds and the bees chat?'

'Something like that . . .' he muttered.

'Really?' Cassie's voice couldn't contain her surprise.

'What? Uh, no,' Ranjit said, as though he'd just been distracted from another thought. 'No, it was nothing. I guess he just wanted to reprimand me, as the elder and supposedly wiser one of us. I guess we were causing a bit of a scene out there.' He gave her a crooked grin.

'I guess so . . .' she whispered, leaning forward to give him a brief, cautious kiss, before pulling a second chair across from an empty desk and sitting down next to him. 'Anyway, sorry I managed to ruin Valentine's Day.'

Ranjit slid a hand across to cover hers. 'You didn't ruin

it. Come on – one thing's for sure, I've never had a date quite like that. I didn't get to properly thank you for the memorable experience!' He smiled.

Cassie knew he was just trying to cheer her up but she couldn't return his grin. 'But that's what the summons is about, isn't it? Carnegie Hall?'

He sighed and nodded solemnly. 'I don't see what else it could be. Cassie . . .' Taking a breath, Ranjit unrolled the scroll and read it through. 'You should know, this is very, very rare. The Elders almost never meet, let alone summon a student. The Council is made up of the most important Few, and their day jobs don't leave much room for governing their own kind. Besides, most of them would find their lives very, ah, awkward, should their secret get out.'

Cassie wrinkled her nose. 'You mean I might recognise some of these Elders?'

'Oh, I'm sure you will. Unless you've never watched the news in your life.'

'Now I'm *definitely* scared.' She rubbed her temples. 'What exactly do they want?'

He studied the bookshelf over her left shoulder. 'To find out what happened, I expect.'

'But I don't *know* what happened, Ranjit. And more importantly, neither does Sir Alric. What are they expecting *me* to tell them?'

'I don't know.' Ranjit squeezed her fingers, but he still wasn't quite meeting her eyes. 'But I'm sure it'll be fine, Cassie. They're not all horrors and despots.'

'Not all,' she repeated dryly.

'You'll be fine,' he said again. 'I'll be there. I'll come with you.'

'You will?' She brightened instantly. 'You can do that?'

'There are a lot of things I can do that you don't know about.' He cocked an eyebrow. 'You have a right to a Supporter. So that's that. I'm not going to let you go alone.' He sounded almost too determined, as though he were trying to convince someone other than just her. She couldn't help feeling a rush of emotion towards him. Standing up, she reached across the pile of books and hugged him. His promise had brought unexpected tears to her eyes and she didn't much want him to see them.

'Thanks, Ranjit.'

'No problem,' he breathed. Then she felt her feet leave the ground, and realised he'd lifted her as if she weighed nothing. Setting her down on his own side of the desk, her body pressed to his, he kissed her properly. It wasn't urgent like last night, just warm and comforting. After a moment he pulled back, with a look that she read as relief. Smiling into his chest, she mumbled,

'You'll definitely be there?'

'I told you. I won't leave you alone.'

No, no he mustn't leave us!

The harsh voice jolted Cassie. She pulled back, shocked.

Are you sure he won't? Do we trust him?

'Of course we do!' she hissed.

'Cassie?' Ranjit frowned down at her. 'What?'

'Sorry. Nothing,' she said hastily. Looking up, she met his anxious gaze.

Can we trust him not to leave us?

Shaking her head to try and loose Estelle, she forced a little laugh, reached up and kissed him quickly. 'I should get going.'

'Don't worry, Cassie. OK? You don't have to worry.'

'Sure.' She smiled a bright fake smile. 'It's only the Council of Elders, right?'

Ranjit laughed quietly. 'Right. See you soon.'

She gave his hand one last squeeze, then hurried away, before Estelle said anything more. Ranjit had told her she didn't have to be worried, and she believed him. She took his word for it. She *did* trust him.

Didn't she?

As Cassie rounded the corner in the stacks she noticed a familiar figure walking away from one of the desks and heading for the door, clutching an armful of files. Jake. She almost called out to him, wanting to harangue him about abandoning Isabella again earlier in the day, but he was already gone. Beneath his desk, though, she could see a single sheet of paper that had slipped to the floor. Cassie bent to pick it up.

It was a page of plain text, a printout from a computer file, that much was clear. The title alone was enough to send shivers right through her:

Highly Classified – Enquiries into the death of Jessica Marie Johnson

But what took Cassie's breath away were the four words that encircled a blue and gold seal at the very top of the page:

Federal Bureau of Investigation

'Jake,' she whispered to herself. 'What the hell have you done?'

CHAPTER FIFTEEN

Insomnia was making the hunger worse. That and stress, Cassie figured. After a sleepless night, Cassie felt so groggy and weak, she skipped a class for the first time in her Darke Academy career. Signor Poldino would accept a sob story about a headache, she decided, groaning as she flopped back on to the pillows. As for confronting Jake about the FBI file, it would just have to wait.

Isabella took a little more convincing than the art master, but as soon as her roommate could be persuaded to leave her in peace and go to class, Cassie blew out a sigh of relief. She rolled over and tugged the melted photographs out from under her mattress. Sitting up cross-legged, she stared at them once more. She could barely comprehend the catalogue of issues confronting her: the melting frames, and then Isabella's bangle; Carnegie Hall and the implications of her new power; the horrible incident with Isabella at Coney Island; Jake and the whole Katerina mess; Ranjit; and, of course, the icing on the cake – a summons from the Council of Elders. Everything seemed to fall back on her, on what she'd *become*. She'd never felt so heartsick and helpless.

The weather wasn't helping. Beyond her window, a weight of dirty snow-cloud lay over the city, and desultory grey flakes drifted down, sticking to the glass. The day looked like she felt.

There was a lot she needed to know, and no one else to ask. Swinging her legs off the bed, she stared out of the plate-glass window. Sir Alric, she thought. He'd promised to research her strange power, and maybe he'd already found more information. She knew she couldn't bear another day without asking, anyway.

When she stepped out of the elevator, the door to his office was open. Unaccountably nervous, she approached. Sir Alric was there in front of his desk, propped against it, talking to someone in the armchair in front of him.

All she could make out of the visitor was the back of his head. It looked familiar – stupidly familiar, because clearly she was mistaken. It couldn't be him – not here in New York. All the same, she felt her heart begin to pound.

It just *couldn't* be him . . . Could it?

She gave her head a quick, hard shake. Instantly Sir

Alric glanced up, catching the movement. In his face shock dawned, and something like anger. He wasn't expecting her. She was interrupting. Cassie raised a tentative hand – partly greeting, partly to indicate that she'd wait – but he didn't acknowledge her.

Instead he snapped his fingers once at someone out of sight, and a secretary stepped into view. 'Sir Alric is busy just now.' The young man gave her an anodyne smile, and closed the door firmly in her face.

Cassie gaped, open-mouthed. 'I'll wait,' she muttered grimly.

There were a few impeccably designed chairs in the corner of the anteroom, but Cassie ignored them and the glossy magazines and the bookshelves. She could only pace back and forth, scowling, as the minutes ticked by. The hideous certainty was growing that she *did* know that visitor. That he *was* who she thought he was. Why else would Sir Alric have reacted the way he did? Fury bubbled up inside her, and she clenched her teeth against it. Maybe she didn't know the wise and kind Sir Alric so well after all.

When the door swung open, she turned, eyes blazing. But it wasn't Sir Alric; it wasn't his secretary.

It was Patrick Malone.

Cassie stared at her old friend, her mentor, her key

worker. Patrick smiled nervously. 'Cassie.'

She took a breath. 'What are you doing here?'

'I . . . I had something to talk to Sir Alric about. It – couldn't wait. Cassie, how are you?' He put out his hand.

She didn't take it. She could feel her fingers trembling, and she didn't want to give away how scared and angry she was. 'I don't know what you're doing, but—'

'Cassandra.' Sir Alric was suddenly standing behind him. 'Patrick was just leaving.'

'Why is he even *here*?'

'Why don't you come in and we can talk about it?'

'Yes, Cassie. Go ahead.' Patrick wasn't smiling any more. 'Sir Alric will explain.' He glanced at the older man.

Cassie frowned, looking from the nervous Patrick to the expressionless features of Sir Alric Darke. She opened her mouth to say no, but then curiosity got the better of her. She nodded silently.

Sir Alric gestured her in as the young secretary escorted Patrick out. He clearly meant to keep them apart, but though the secretary moved swiftly past Cassie, not even giving her a glance, Patrick halted to hug her. Stiffly she endured it, determined not to hug him back. She was already feeling the painful sting of secrets she didn't know.

Sir Alric closed the door firmly as soon as Patrick was beyond it.

'Yes, Cassandra. Why don't you take a seat?' Sir Alric sat down behind his desk, but swivelled his chair forty-five degrees so that he was in profile, staring out across the city skyline. His dismissive coolness was unsettling: she'd expected a little contrition. She had to take another breath before she could speak, and she remained standing.

'Patrick.' She licked her lips and swallowed. 'What is he doing here?'

'Why wouldn't he come? He's been trying to contact you since the beginning of term.' Sir Alric swivelled his chair to face her. 'There was no reply, it seems. Naturally he was worried about you.'

Cassie chewed the inside of her cheek.

'His messages didn't reach you, I take it?'

'They reached me,' she muttered.

'I see.'

'Look, I didn't want to talk to him, OK? I wasn't ready.'

Shutting his eyes, he massaged the bridge of his nose. 'Why not?'

'Because he *knows*. About this school. About everything. About the Few. Doesn't he?'

Once again Sir Alric turned to look out at the city. 'Yes.'

'And he knows I'm . . . Few?'

'Yes. That's why he's been worried. Did that not occur to you, Cassandra?'

She bit her lip to stop herself swearing at him. The arrogance of the man! Was he being obtuse on purpose or did he really not understand how this made her feel?

'How does Patrick know?'

Sir Alric gave a heavy sigh. 'He knows, Cassandra, because he was a student here himself.'

Cassie sat back in her chair. For long seconds she couldn't speak.

'How do you think he knew about us? Why do you think he'd suggest you apply to this school, of all places?'

'Yes, why?' Cassie stood up sharply. 'Why *would* he? He knew about you, and the Few? He knew everything about this place – that's what you're telling me – and yet he still sent me here?' There was a pain in her chest that was suffocating.

'Sit down, Cassandra.' Sir Alric shot her a glance, then turned away yet again. Funny, she thought bitterly as she subsided into the chair, how he couldn't seem to face her.

'I'm waiting,' she said softly.

He steepled his fingers and turned to her properly at last. 'Patrick sent you because he knew what was on offer here: what you could gain. He knew you'd meet our educational standards, he knew you'd benefit enormously from time at the Academy. Believe me, he thought long and hard before he sent you here. But send you he did.'

Cassie felt dizzy. She put her hands to the sides of her head. 'And look what happened to me,' she whispered. 'How could he?'

'Because he didn't anticipate this. None of us did. He thought it was impossible, that there was no chance of you becoming Few. He made me promise to choose your roommate wisely, to give you the best companion possible. I gave him that promise very happily. That's something that has worked out for the best, I think?'

She rubbed her forehead. 'Yes. Yes, that did.'

'Patrick, you see, roomed with a Few member. Erik was a fine member of the Few and an even finer human being. Patrick respected him enormously, and the feeling was mutual. Just like you and Isabella, Erik refused to deceive Patrick. He fed on him with Patrick's full knowledge and consent, and no harm was ever done. Their relationship was as perfect as it gets between Few and life-source.'

The casual way he said it sent a buzz of horror down Cassie's spine.

'Patrick knew you'd be safe. With the best of girls as your roommate, you'd be protected, you'd be privileged, and he knew from his own experience that no harm would come to you. Above all, he thought that there was no chance – not the slightest possibility – of you ever becoming Few yourself. Patrick too was a scholarship boy. He knew it was supposed to be impossible.'

'And then along came Estelle,' whispered Cassie. Her whole being felt numb.

Sir Alric nodded solemnly. 'Is there anything else you wish to know?'

She shook her head slowly. 'Nothing. I don't want to know anything else about that. Except . . .'

He watched her in silence, waiting.

'This guy Erik. Patrick's roommate. You said he *was* a fine human being.'

'Oh yes. Erik Ragnarsson is dead.'

Cassie let that sink in. No, she wouldn't ask anything more. She didn't want to know.

'I thought it was best that I explain, rather than Patrick. Given your . . .' he paused, '*volatile* state. Would you like to speak to him now?'

Violently she shook her head. 'No! No, I don't want to see him.'

'Very well.' Sir Alric inclined his head. 'Then all that's left, Miss Bell, is to tell me why you came to see me in the first place.'

God. She'd almost forgotten. With a shaking hand, Cassie drew the gilt-edged scroll from her pocket. The expensive parchment was barely crumpled. In light of what had just happened, the summons seemed so much less important. She hardly cared about it any more.

No. No, she *had* to care. She had to know. Cassie gritted her teeth. 'Do you know anything about this?'

Sir Alric gave the summons a casual glance. 'I knew you'd received it.'

'You knew? Did you know it was coming? Before then, I mean?'

'Yes.'

Cassie stared down at the parchment in her hand. 'Did you tell them? The Elders, I mean. About me?'

'Of course.'

He sounded so reasonable she wanted to strike him.

'Why?'

Sir Alric smiled. 'Since the events at Carnegie Hall, I have spoken to several of my colleagues on the Council to see if they could offer any explanation for the powers you manifested.'

'And could they?' Cassie swallowed hard. 'What did you find out?'

'Nothing. I can't give you any further information I'm afraid, Cassandra. I've studied several volumes. Nothing so far has come to light.'

'Then why does the Council want to see me? What aren't you telling me?'

In the silence it was only Cassie who fidgeted, screwing

the scroll anxiously in her hands. Why did Sir Alric seem so perfectly composed, so perfectly calm? She was beginning to hate him. Her heart rate began to increase as she flushed with irritation.

'I believe I have told you everything I can.' Sir Alric stood up. 'Will there be anything else, Cassandra?'

He was *so* tall. Power just radiated out of him. She remembered thinking that, the first time she'd met him. How impressed she'd been. How intimidated. Not any more.

Not any more!

She rose to her feet. 'You can't control me.'

'What did you say?' Sir Alric's voice was dangerously calm.

She drew herself up instinctively. 'I'm stronger than you think, Alric,' she hissed.

His eyes narrowed. A muscle below his eye tightened.

'*Do not underestimate me!*' Her lips drew back from her teeth.

'Cassandra . . .' Sir Alric's voice was a low rumble, but his expression was wary.

The room was red again. But her crimson-tinged vision was not so frightening this time. It meant power. She liked it. How dare he treat her this way! Fury tingled in her spine, trembled like an aura outside her body.

'Cassandra!'

She didn't reply. Instead, she laughed. Wildly she looked round the room. It was like him. All elegance. All taste. All control! She'd show him . . .

Reaching out, her aura of power spread across the room. Through the stained-glass shade of an exquisite designer table lamp, the bulb glowed brighter – then brighter still. The light changed colour, even as it intensified. Now the unbearable glare was blood-red and laser-bright, brilliant with energy. Sir Alric gave an exclamation of horror, and reached for it.

Too late. The bulb exploded into fine glass rain, showering his hand and arm.

'*Cassandra!*'

His tone had changed entirely. There was anger in it now, a menacing snarl. Glaring at him, she saw his own eyes turn fiery red, first at the pupils, then sparking outwards so that the whole eyeball glowed scarlet. God, but he was strong! The light of his spirit burned in his chest like a dark sun.

That was how she looked. Suddenly she knew it.

Monstrous.

Cassie ground her teeth so hard it hurt. The aura around her wavered.

Hurt him! Hurt him! How dare *he treat us so!*

Cassie shut her eyes tight.

HURT HIM!

'NO!' she snarled. Her fists tightened; she could feel her fingernails digging into her palms. Sir Alric stood absolutely still, but she knew he was coiled and ready.

Ready to defend himself? Attack?

Attack!

No!

Slowly, trembling and sucking in deep gulps of air, she felt her fists unclench, her muscles relax. As she closed her eyes and opened them again, the red filter dissipated and she could see him clearly once more. His own eyes remained red for a moment, then faded slowly back to their normal grey.

'Control yourself,' he murmured. It was still a growl, but a less aggressive one. 'Good.'

Without taking his eyes off her, Sir Alric brushed at the glittering shards of glass on his sleeve. He'd cut his finger, Cassie noticed. There was blood. She set her jaw, trying to suppress the pleasure she felt at this.

Breathing hard, she waited until she was sure she could walk without trembling. Then she turned, shaking, and walked from the room, closing the door firmly behind her.

CHAPTER SIXTEEN

I can help you, my dearest. You're weak. I don't want you to sicken, my sweet Cassandra. Let me help you. Let us be together. Don't leave me out here, not when I can save you. We can save each other . . .

'Oh, God,' mumbled Cassie. 'Estelle . . .'

'Cassie!' Isabella tugged at her arm. 'You are dreaming again. Talking to yourself. Wake *up!*'

Cassie forced her eyes open. Low sunlight slanted into the room from the huge window overlooking Central Park. It had been hours since she had stumbled down from Sir Alric's office, weak with hunger. Isabella must be back from class.

'Isabella?'

'Cassie, what's wrong? What can I do?'

As usual, her roommate was fizzing with energy, and Cassie found herself leaning hungrily towards her.

Stretching out a clutching hand, she missed Isabella by a New York mile, and tumbled clumsily to the floor.

'Cassie? Cassie!' Isabella crouched beside her. 'Oh, Cassie, you're ill! Here, let me help you—'

'No!' Cassie scrambled back, pressing herself between the bed and the nightstand, and raised her hand, palm outward, to keep her friend at bay. 'No, Isabella, don't! I'm – I think I need to feed.'

Isabella hesitated, blinking at Cassie's outstretched palm. Then she clasped it, hauling Cassie to her feet and gripping her shoulders.

Cassie endured it, rigid with terror. Any moment now . . . any moment . . .

Isabella cupped Cassie's face in her hands, a serious look on her own. 'So you should feed. Come on.'

Cassie stared as her roommate extended her arms. 'N-no!'

'Cassie, you look *terrible*. Please?' Isabella pushed her wrists into Cassie's hands, but she pulled away quickly. Isabella shook her head, concerned and angry. 'Look at you! Your skin is like paper. Your eyes are dull. You should not have left it so long. Come. We'll go to Sir Alric. He'll help.'

'No way.' Cassie shook her head rapidly. 'No way, I'm not going to him.'

'But, Cassie, why?'

'I'm not – I'll explain later.' Cassie put her hands to her throat. 'Oh, God, Isabella. I'm so *thirsty*.'

'Here, take this.' Isabella lifted her bedside carafe to Cassie's lips. She gulped desperately, but it wasn't helping. 'Wait here. Do not move.' Clasping Cassie's hands tightly around the carafe, she fled from the room.

Cassie had drained it, refilled it and was swigging great gulps from it once more when Isabella returned. With her was Ayeesha, who stopped dead when she laid eyes on Cassie.

'My God! Cassie, what's wrong with you?' she exclaimed.

'She needs to feed.' Isabella folded her arms. 'Now. Ayeesha, can you help us? She's only done it once before.'

'*Once?* Cassie, you've fed only once?' The Bajan girl's eyes were wide with horror. 'What have you been doing to yourself?'

'She's nervous about feeding from me,' said Isabella grimly. 'She's been holding back.'

Ayeesha did a double take as the realisation of what Isabella had been saying dawned on her. Staring at her for a few seconds, she turned and gave Cassie an intent meaningful look. 'Don't you think *Isabella* should have a drink too?'

For a moment, Cassie couldn't think what she was on

about. Then she remembered the drink the Few gave their roommates, to make them forget the feeding.

''S OK, Ayeesha,' she mumbled weakly. 'She knows. Agreed to it.'

'Really?' Ayeesha still looked wary. 'Perhaps we should call Sir Alric . . .'

'No!' Cassie's voice was a cracked rasp.

'OK. I'll help you, then. Can you remember what you've been taught?'

Isabella nodded quickly for both of them. 'Yes. Cassie – come on.' She stretched her arms towards Cassie once more, and through her haze of confusion Cassie was sure she saw her friend's hands trembling ever so slightly.

Ayeesha patted Isabella's shoulder reassuringly. 'Now, Cassie. Take hold of her.'

Cassie staggered groggily to her feet. Isabella smiled a little nervously and closed her eyes as Cassie's thumb and forefinger tightened around her wrists.

She could feel Isabella's blood pulsing underneath her fingertips, and the breath rushing in and out of her roommate's parted lips. She lurched forward, closing the gap between them, but then felt a warning hand on her arm.

'Careful,' murmured Ayeesha. 'Keep control.'

'What if I can't?' Cassie felt wild.

'I'll stop you, believe me. But you *can* keep control. You know you can, you've done it before. Take it slowly.'

As she closed her eyes and took a deep breath, Cassie felt a surge of violent hunger. But Ayeesha's fingers tightened on her arm, and the physical reminder helped her keep a hold of herself.

Cassie felt a bolt of sheer, sudden ecstasy as the endless breath began to move from Isabella, filling her own lungs and fizzing out through her whole body. Isabella's life-force was tremendous – so vital! All that effervescent, unstoppable energy . . . It raced through her veins, raising the hair on her scalp. She almost laughed, feeling giddy. Blood throbbed in her ears, and she felt fierce and alive again. Gripping her friend's wrists tighter, she sucked the life-force in, revelling in the rush.

A sound momentarily distracted her.

A knock on the door?

Cassie's eyes opened and she glanced aside for an instant, still drawing Isabella's life-force, faster now . . .

'Who is it?' Ayeesha called, frowning. Her grip on Cassie's arm loosened a little as her attention was diverted.

'It's me. Jake.' A pause. 'Who's *that*?'

Isabella's eyes flew wide open, horrified. Cassie saw the shocked reaction, but she didn't stop sucking, drawing that breath through the space between them and into her lungs.

'Wait a moment, Jake,' called Ayeesha.

No, of course Jake mustn't know. Ayeesha mustn't let him in. Somewhere in her delirium, Cassie realised she should tell her that. Stop and tell her now, right now.

But she couldn't stop, not just yet . . .

Quick! Quick!

Isabella was pulling now, tugging to try to escape Cassie's grip. She was panicking about Jake, of course.

Never mind him! Never mind any of that. Keep going!

Suddenly the panic and terror in Isabella's eyes was different. She was flailing, struggling, and a horrible gasping noise was coming from deep in her throat.

Make her shut up and be still!

The girl was struggling now. The veins in her throat throbbed. But it wasn't enough. She'd have to take more . . .

No! No!

YES! Give me more of her! We're HUNGRY, Cassandra! Lock your mouth to hers and take it ALL!

NO! I can't . . .

KEEP HOLD OF HER! DON'T LET GO!

Estelle, no – she's my best friend!

She's not your best friend. I AM!

174

'Cassie? Cassie!' Ayeesha's voice cut into her brain as her attention snapped back to the feeding pair. 'Cassie, stop it this minute!'

Ignore her!

Fingers bit into Cassie's arm, tearing at her. Anger surged, and she sucked more life to compensate. Red fury fizzed through her.

'CASSIE!' Ayeesha's fingers dug hard into her wrists, hurting her.

That was when the door burst open.

'What the hell?'

Shocked out of her trance, Cassie broke her hold. Isabella stumbled, gasping, to one knee. Then she fell back on to her elbows.

'Enough, for God's sake. Enough.' Ayeesha pulled Cassie away from Isabella and shook her angrily.

'What's going on? Isabella? Cassie!'

All three of them turned towards Jake – Ayeesha embarrassed, Isabella pale and shaky, Cassie still buzzing with energy. Her fingertips tingled, her brain tingled. She felt like she could spring up through the roof.

Jake's face was a mask of incredulous fury. 'You . . . fed on her? That's what you were doing? You FED ON HER?'

Jake was paler than Cassie had ever seen him, his fists clenched. She wiped her mouth, breathing hard.

'How *could* you?' His words were barely above a rumble in his throat, dripping venom.

'Jake, that's enough!' Isabella was breathless, scrambling weakly to her feet.

'Isabella? Are you OK?'

Isabella forced a shaky smile, rubbing her wrists. 'Fine. Jake, I'm fine. Don't fret.'

'But . . . D'you realise what she was . . .' Jake's voice faded and he slumped against the wall as the reality sunk in. 'My God. Isabella – you agreed to this?'

'Yes. Yes, Jake. Look, I'm sorry, I . . .'

He turned on Cassie, raging. 'How could you? After Jess? After you saw what Keiko did to Alice? You did this to your *friend*?'

'Keiko? Keiko was not like the rest of us!' Ayeesha interjected angrily. 'Keiko was sadistic! She *liked* to hurt when she fed. And Alice didn't remember anyway!'

'What difference does that make? Stay out of this!' yelled Jake. 'You're just a monster like – like *she* is!' He jabbed a finger at Cassie.

Cassie ignored him. Suddenly he didn't matter. All that mattered was . . .

'Isabella. Are you *sure* you're OK? Did . . . did I hurt you?'

'Seriously. I'm all right, Cassie. Jake, please . . .'

'To hell with it, Isabella. You don't care what I think, what this means to me . . .'

'Jake, that isn't true!'

'Oh, really? You let this *lifesucker* feed off you and you weren't even going to let me know? Fine. At least I know where I stand.'

'Jake, please!' Isabella reached out a pleading hand. 'She didn't hurt me. She won't ever hurt me!'

His voice was a hiss. 'You can say that to me with a straight face? Forget it, Isabella. But don't forget – don't *ever* forget – what they did to my sister.'

With that, he turned his back and stormed out of the room.

CHAPTER SEVENTEEN

If she'd felt bad before, she was in a pit of misery now. Cassie had a horrible feeling she was never going to see Jake again. She was longing for him to walk into the classroom, yet dreading it. He was never going to forgive her. Never.

She could barely even smile at Ranjit when he arrived and sat beside her. She could feel his perplexed glances, but she couldn't take her eyes off the door. Her heart skipped a beat every time it opened, but when the maths class started there was still no sign of Jake. Words and figures floated in and out of her ears, unheeded. By the time class was over, she was so preoccupied she gathered her books together and walked out without a thought.

'Cassie!' Ranjit was hurrying after her. 'Hey. What's up? Have I done something wrong?'

She hesitated. 'You? No, of course not.'

'So what's wrong?'

Turning, she studied him properly. His handsome face did look anxious. 'Sorry. Ranjit, I'm sorry. It's Jake.'

Ranjit's face took on a guarded expression. 'What about him?'

'He caught me feeding off Isabella on Friday. We haven't seen him since. He hasn't been to class or his room.'

Cassie bit her lip. Saying it out loud reminded her how awful the situation was.

'Oh, hell.'

'Quite.' Unhappily she shifted from foot to foot. 'First Katerina shows up again, then this . . .'

'Hey, listen, maybe it's for the best if he cools off away from the Academy for a bit, clears his head. I mean, he must have had some inkling about you and Isabella? It can't have been *too* much of a shock. He just needs some time to adjust.'

Cassie felt her hackles rise. 'Adjust? I can't really see that happening. Did he adjust to the knowledge of his sister having the life sucked out of her?' Something burned in her eyes, a pinprick heat that was already expanding.

Ranjit rubbed his forehead with his fist. 'Sorry. Sorry, that was tactless. I didn't mean—'

'It was a stupid thing to say,' she snapped.

'*OK*. Cassie, he'll come around. He's got to.'

'Yeah? You don't know anything about Jake.' Blinking furiously to get rid of the reddish tinge in her vision, Cassie turned and walked swiftly away.

Once she was out of Ranjit's immediate vicinity, the heat in her eyes subsided and she could think straight again. For a moment she thought he wasn't going to follow, and guilt and remorse hit her. Then she heard his footsteps hurrying after her.

'Cassie, please, I'm sorry. I'm trying to help.'

She halted, afraid to look at him. She sighed. 'I know. Ranjit, I'm sorry too. I don't know why I snapped. I'm just so stressed out, with this Council meeting coming up, and now Jake . . .'

'It's OK.' He put a hand on her shoulder, then touched her face gently. She took his hand and led him into a quieter corner.

'Well,' she said, looking up uncertainly at Ranjit's handsome face, 'there's something else about Jake. He knows Katerina is in New York. He's been trying to find her. He wants justice for Jess. I think he might have hacked the FBI computer system to get some files about her death. He has some sort of crazy notion of putting Katerina on trial.'

180

Ranjit froze. 'He did *what*? Cassie, this is serious. You have to tell Sir Alric. We need to deal with this before Jake does something we'll regret.'

'Something *we'll* regret? It's him I'm worried about. Look, I know you don't have a lot of friends, so maybe you don't get it—' Cassie stopped short as she saw his expression change, hurt briefly flickering across his face. She took a deep breath. God, what was she saying? The last thing she wanted to do was hurt Ranjit. She mustn't get angry, not now. She just needed to make sure he understood. Lowering her voice, she started again. 'I didn't mean that. I'm sorry. But, Ranjit, please, this is important. You cannot tell *anyone* about Jake. Please. I just need to talk to him. Explain things.'

'Cassie, this goes beyond friendship. If Jake gets caught hacking the FBI system and ends up talking about the Few and the Academy – it could have severe implications for *all* of us.' He stared at her meaningfully.

'I don't care about that. What happens to the Academy is nothing to do with this.'

Ranjit shook his head. He seemed to be making some effort to stay calm too. 'Cassie, the fate of the Academy involves you as well. You need to remember that.'

Cassie took both of his hands. 'Just a little time. If I can't persuade him to drop it then, OK, we'll tell Sir Alric.'

She held his gaze, and his eyes were a tumult of emotion.

'OK, Cassie. I won't say anything. I swear.'

She met his reassuring gaze, and exhaled deeply.

Are you sure that's the best course of action, Cassandra, my dear? We must do what we can keep him on our side. We mustn't let him get away . . .

Cassie pretended not to hear Estelle's words. She'd had about enough of her interjections. 'Thank you, Ranjit. Thanks a lot. Look, I'll see you tomorrow, OK?'

'Yes. I'll meet you at your room an hour before the Council meeting.'

'Yes. Great, yes of course.' This time it was tears that pricked her eyes. How could she even entertain the thought of doubting him? Cassie leaned forward quickly and kissed him.

He caught her as she drew away, and pulled her back, pressing his lips more firmly against hers. As her heart looped the loop, she shut her eyes and indulged herself in his touch – but not too much. When he pulled away and smiled his goodbye, she paused for a moment, stunned, but pleasantly so. They *could* do this. Whatever was off balance, whatever had been causing their extremes of emotion, they were working it out. They could do this.

That was when she caught sight of Sir Alric.

He'd been watching them, she thought, as a chill went

down her spine. Her sense of wellbeing quickly dispersed, the look on his face cloudy, but calculating.

'Cassandra. Can I speak with you a moment?' Sir Alric started towards her.

Oh, no. She had enough to handle right now, and she'd had enough of disapproval. Her relationship with Ranjit was absolutely none of his business. With a defiant glare and a shake of her head, Cassie turned very deliberately and walked away.

Out of the corner of her eye, Cassie watched Isabella thumbing her phone under her desk. She was at it again. Madame Lefevre was going to spot her soon, and then she'd be for it. You could push Madame so far, and then no further.

Still Cassie could understand Isabella taking the risk. They had heard nothing from Jake since the weekend: no phone call, no message. Her friend's expression was growing increasingly desperate with every failed call.

'. . . and so we see that Simone de Beauvoir has much to say about humanity and relationships, even to the world of the twenty-first century, which is why we should listen, hear what she is telling us, because we will gain so much more than we will learn from *semi-literate texting throughout our class.*'

Uh-oh. Cassie gulped, but Isabella hadn't even heard Madame's warning. When the woman stalked to her side and snapped her fingers for the phone, Isabella almost jumped out of her skin.

'You may have it back after class,' said Madame Lefevre curtly. 'On this occasion.'

Miserable, visibly reluctant, Isabella passed her phone into Madame's waiting palm, and caught Cassie's eye. Cassie could only try to send her psychic messages of sympathy. Madame wasn't the strictest teacher in the school; Isabella had been really blatant.

Still, Cassie didn't know why Madame Lefevre had bothered to confiscate the phone; it wasn't as if Isabella concentrated any harder on Simone de Beauvoir for the remaining twenty minutes. She wrung her fingers beneath her desk, staring unseeing at her textbook, and shooting anxious glances out of the window at the Manhattan skyline. She certainly wasn't learning anything.

Cassie waited for Isabella while she endured her after-class dressing-down. Her fingers were twitching, and when Madame finally gave her the phone back she rushed from class, dialling frantically.

'*Call failed.* Again! Why is his phone switched off?'

'I don't know.' What else was there to say? She could

hardly tell Isabella not to worry. Jake had been beyond furious. 'I'm so sorry, Isabella.'

'It's not your fault.' Isabella patted her arm. 'It's mine. I said you could feed, didn't I? It was I who panicked. And all because . . .' Tears sprang to her eyes. 'All because I insisted on keeping it from Jake. I didn't want you to lie to *me*, but then I lied to him. You see? It's my fault.'

That made Cassie feel even worse. 'Isabella, you mustn't—'

'I tell you, he must have gone home to Queens.' Her friend's gaze was distant. 'I just don't know why he won't even speak to me. And I'm afraid if I turn up at his parents' house, he'll just get even more angry . . . Maybe they won't even let me in.'

'Wait, Isabella, you want to go to his house? I don't know if that's a good idea right now.' She was panicking a little – Cassie had hoped to get a chance to speak to Jake before Isabella got to him. Her roommate still wasn't aware that Jake knew Katerina was in New York. She needed to know exactly what Jake was planning, and didn't want Isabella any more involved than she had to be. She owed the girl that much.

'Maybe it's not. But I have to try, don't I?' Isabella came to a halt, breathing hard. She swiped at her eyes. 'Still, I'm really worried. I mean, his parents were not happy about him coming back to school. Of course that made him feel bad. But he came back anyway, and that was at least partly for me. And now the feeding – and me lying – that has been the tripping point. Yes? He has left the school and gone home. And I think he won't ever come back! All my fault!' she wailed.

'Isabella, calm down. He'll be back.'

'No, Cassie. He won't come back on his own. If only I can talk to him, say I'm sorry, make him understand.'

'Isabella . . .'

'After school. I'm going to see him. That's it, that's the only solution.'

Cassie sighed. 'That's what you were thinking about instead of Simone de Beauvoir.'

'I'll make it up to Simone later.' The fire was back in Isabella's eyes. 'But in the meantime, I think she'd understand.'

Cassie shook her head. 'OK. Well you're not going alone. I'm coming with you.'

Cassie glanced at the afternoon sky, still as crystal-clear and stunning as it had been when they crossed the Brooklyn Bridge and gaped at the view of the city, but now a covering of icy grey clouds were hovering on the horizon.

'It's going to snow soon. You're sure you know where—'

'There!' Isabella leaned forward to the taxi driver. 'Right down this street.'

Cassie peered out of the cab window at the dilapidated buildings. 'I have a feeling they're not going to be happy to see us.'

'I don't care if they are or not. I must speak to Jake.' Isabella flicked through her leather Gucci organiser. 'Now, let me find the exact number . . . Ah, here! Here, driver, please!' Her sudden shriek made the driver start and growl a curse. He pulled the cab to a halt, and Isabella quickly handed over the fare and leaped out. Cassie followed closely behind her.

'Hold the door, please,' Isabella called as an elderly man exited the apartment building. He looked a little dubious, but as Isabella approached and smiled sweetly, he nodded and obliged.

'What number is it?' Cassie asked.

'Five-eighteen,' said Isabella, her face now serious again.

The building was several storeys high and there didn't seem to be an elevator. This was definitely a different New York. The stairwell smelled of cooking and the paint was peeling in a few corners. The walls were thin enough for

Cassie's heightened hearing to pick up a couple rowing on the third floor. It was a world away from the Darke Academy building, but it felt somehow friendly: noisy, warm and homely.

Outside Jake's parents' apartment were well-tended plants and a scuffed Welcome mat. 'If only that were true,' Cassie muttered.

Isabella ignored her. Taking a deep breath, she rattled the brass knocker, and almost immediately the cheerful sky-blue door jerked open.

'Honey, thank God you're back – oh!' The woman staring at Isabella had obviously been expecting someone else, because she took a breath and closed her mouth mid-sentence.

She was very good-looking – well, thought Cassie as she remembered Jake, of course she was – but there were shadows under her red-rimmed eyes, and her face was drawn with anxiety. Her tawny hair was pulled back in a ponytail, and her teeth bit into her lip.

'Sorry. I thought you were— Oh my . . .' Jake's mother tailed off again as her nervous gaze found Cassie. Her eyes lingered on her for an uncomfortable moment, as if she couldn't believe what she was seeing. Then she shook her head. 'I apologise. It's just you . . . you look so much like my daughter.'

Cassie found herself taking a step back. She dropped her eyes, swallowing hard. 'I'm Jake's friend, Cassie. And this is Isabella.'

Recognition, followed by discomfort, seemed to flicker across Mrs Johnson's face. 'Oh. Isabella. Jake's girlfriend . . . He's mentioned you.'

'Janice?' came a deep voice from further inside the apartment. 'Who is it?'

A moment later, a man appeared at Mrs Johnson's side. He was unmistakably Jake's father: tall and handsome, but his large brown eyes too were shadowed with worry. He also seemed surprised to find Cassie and Isabella standing at his door.

'That's right, I'm Jake's girlfriend,' Isabella continued. She took a breath and extended her hand. 'It's good to meet you, Mrs Johnson. Mr Johnson. Uh, is there any chance we could come in?'

Flustered, Jake's mother touched Isabella's outstretched hand briefly, glancing over her shoulder at her husband. Then her eyes were drawn helplessly back to Cassie.

'No, I . . . This isn't a very good time, I'm sorry . . .'

Isabella stepped forward. 'Please, Mrs Johnson. We won't take up much of your time. We just want to speak to Jake for a second. Is he here?'

Mrs Johnson gave a shaky sigh. 'No, he isn't. He barely

left the house all weekend. He was working on his computer the whole time. Then, this afternoon, he raced out like a tornado. He said he had found what he was looking for, but he had to go back to the Academy. Something about being traced. Listen, what's going on? Jake wouldn't tell us anything, but he was obviously worried about you, Isabella. He seemed to think that you were in some sort of danger – that the same thing that happened to Jessica might happen to you.'

'He said that?' Isabella swallowed.

'Yes!' snapped Mr Johnson. 'What did he mean? Look, if you girls know something, you should tell us.'

Cassie glanced at Isabella, but her face was suddenly calm as she replied, 'I'm sorry, Mr and Mrs Johnson. Jake and I had an argument, and I think he may have misunderstood a few things. I think we'd better go. Sorry to have troubled you.'

She gave a polite smile and turned to leave before Jake's parents could say anything more. Cassie heard the Johnsons' door slam shut as they made their way downstairs and into the slushy street. Wet snow was falling again. When she glanced up at the window of the apartment, Cassie saw the twitch of a blind, caught a last glimpse of Mr Johnson's suspicious face.

'We need a cab,' said Isabella, scanning the streets for

yellow paintwork, once again determined. 'We need to find Jake. Something's not right, something more than just seeing you feeding on me. Why else would he leave his parents' apartment again?'

'Isabella, I have to tell you something . . .' Cassie's voice caught in her throat, but there was nothing for it. Secrets and lies had got them into this mess. There was no point keeping things hidden any longer. Cassie took a deep breath.

'I think we may not be the only ones looking for him.'

CHAPTER EIGHTEEN

Isabella visibly blanched, then let out a piercing wail.

'The *FBI*?'

The cab driver threw her an irritated look via his rear-view mirror.

'Shhh!'

'Cassie, I can't believe you didn't tell me this!'

Cassie took a deep breath, trying to avoid her friend's incredulous gaze. She cleared her throat uncomfortably.

'I'm sorry, Isabella. I should have told you about finding that printout, but I didn't want to worry you until I'd had a chance to speak to Jake myself. But then he walked in on us and it all just—'

Isabella's hand suddenly closed around her own. She realised they were shaking.

'OK, Cassie. It doesn't matter now. All that matters is that we talk to Jake and find out what's going on.'

They had managed to catch a cab after ten minutes of desperate flagging, but it felt like an age until they finally pulled up to the Academy. As they walked into the atrium, Cassie glanced back through the glass doors and her heart stopped. Stepping out of a silver saloon car were two burly, stone-faced men in identical suits and dark glasses. They barged past the girls and headed for the elevators. Their suits were cut generously at the armpits, Cassie noticed. She'd seen enough television cop shows to know that meant shoulder holsters.

'Johnson's room is on the third floor,' muttered one of the men to his associate as they pushed the elevator call button.

'Shit,' Cassie whispered, nodding towards the men. 'Isabella, we have to get to Jake's room *now*.'

'Let's take the stairs.' Isabella was already breaking into a run. They took the steps two at a time, and arrived, panting, at Jake's room in a matter of seconds.

'Jake!' Isabella banged on his door so hard Cassie thought she might break it. 'Jake, are you there? Please, Jake, open up.'

Almost to their surprise, the door swung open. Jake stood before them, his expression stormy.

'Forget it, Isabella, I can't talk now.'

'Jake, listen—' Cassie began.

'To you? No, thanks.' Jake made to move past them.

'The FBI,' she blurted. 'They know you've been accessing their files.'

'I know that,' snapped Jake. 'They traced me to my parents' house this afternoon. That's why I came back here.'

'Yeah, well I think they're here now.'

Jake froze. 'What?'

'Please,' Cassie continued, 'I don't think we have much time—'

Before she could finish, the elevator pinged, and footsteps began echoing down the hallway.

'Someone's coming,' Isabella hissed. 'Jake!'

'Get out of here, both of you. I'll deal with this.'

The footsteps were getting closer, approaching the corner. Cassie grabbed Isabella's arm.

'He's right. Isabella, come on!' she said, beginning to drag her friend off in the opposite direction from the advancing steps.

'Jake . . .' Isabella started, reaching out briefly to touch his hand before Cassie pulled her away, back into the emergency stairwell. From there, they heard the footsteps reach Jake's door.

'Jacob Johnson?' intoned a deep, stern voice. 'Federal Bureau of Investigation. You're under arrest.'

Cassie knew nothing would snap Isabella out of her desolate mood, but since the afternoon's events she had refused to eat a bite and wouldn't step outside of their room. What she needed was food; Cassie knew just how bad things looked through a film of hunger . . .

The paper bag full of bagels was warm in her gloved hands, and it smelled delicious. She was on the point of dashing through the Academy's glass doors when she spotted a familiar figure lounging against a limousine on the corner of the block.

Richard – she'd recognise his silhouette anywhere.

He saw Cassie at the same moment and straightened up. The way the streetlight shone, it was impossible to make out his expression, but the car instantly drew away from the kerb, seeming to purr with malevolent satisfaction as it passed her.

Cassie froze. The windows were tinted, but one of them was rolled down – the one Richard had been bent to – and the car's occupant was in no hurry to raise it again. As the glass slid upwards, Cassie stared. A face smiled back at her with absolute chilling coldness: a pale, lovely face. One hand lifted lazily to push back silvery-blonde hair, revealing the familiar brutal scar. Then the black window shut, silently, and the car was gone into the East Side night.

'Cassie!' Richard's call was panicked.

Dropping the bag of bagels, Cassie stormed towards him, red mist shrouding her vision in an instant.

'Cassie, look, it's not what you think—'

'Just when I think you can't disgust me any further, Richard,' she snarled, 'you find some new low to sink to.'

Cassie felt the heat prickling up her neck as the peculiar shimmering feeling spread out from her, just like at Carnegie Hall.

Yes, Cassandra, it's been too long since you let us play . . .

'Cassie?' Richard's voice was uncertain now, but his stance was wary, poised for defence.

She knew that if she looked at Richard a moment longer, she would do something they would both regret. With a massive effort, she turned away and the shimmering faded. 'You're not worth it.'

She said it quite softly, to herself. But she had a feeling he heard her anyway.

CHAPTER NINETEEN

Ranjit was late.

Cassie checked her watch for the twentieth time. Isabella had finally decided to go for a walk to clear her head. Their room was still and silent as Cassie paced its length.

She was due to meet with the Elders in thirty-five minutes and she'd have liked a bit of time to talk it over with Ranjit first, settle her nerves. At least she wasn't fretting too much over her impending confrontation; she was too anxious about where Ranjit was now. She'd tried to get hold of him to fill him in on what had happened with Jake, but he wasn't answering his phone, and wasn't in his room.

It wasn't like him to break his word. Had something happened? She felt a little chill of fear. The way things had been going lately . . .

She glanced at her watch again, at the minutes ticking

inexorably by. Maybe she'd done something, said something? They'd had the argument about how to deal with Jake yesterday, but Ranjit had moved on from that, he'd been fine about it. Besides, now that issue had kind of been taken care of for them. And the way he'd kissed her, there can't have been any confusion about where they stood.

But he was such a puzzle. And kind of inscrutable sometimes. Could he have found out something about her power, something that was delaying him? In which case, he could at least phone. All that talk of being there for her, but where the hell was he then, the one time she really needed him? Cassie felt the stirrings of anger.

Perhaps your hold on him isn't tight enough, my dear. What did I tell you . . . ?

'Not now, Estelle,' Cassie said through gritted teeth.

Her fury was dissipated by a rap at the door. Cassie gasped in relief. All right, now she could forgive and forget: he'd made it, and she didn't care that he was late. She flung the door open.

Blinking, Cassie stared. Instead of Ranjit, she was facing the squat, brutish porter Marat. The one who'd taken such delight in holding her down while Sir Alric injected her with the Tears. And she had a feeling his pleasure hadn't been in saving her bacon.

Marat jerked his head and stood back.

'Now? I have to come now?' Cassie looked in panic at her watch.

Marat nodded silently and there seemed no point arguing. With a last regretful look at her room, Cassie tugged on her coat, closed the door and followed him. Ranjit would have to catch up. He probably knew where they were going.

Which reminded her. 'Where are we going?'

No response.

'Well, is it far?'

The porter shook his head slowly.

'You're a mine of information.'

As she followed Marat out of the Academy's doors and on to Fifth Avenue, a blast of cold air chilled her to the core.

Ranjit, she thought, please come on . . .

Snow was falling again, but it wasn't the thick, soft flakes that at least left the city looking beautiful. This was the driving half-sleet, turning to slush almost as soon as it fell. The wind was biting. Cassie didn't want to hang about; she climbed into the black car as soon as Marat opened the door, huddling into Isabella's vicuna jersey for comfort.

Marat wasn't kidding about *not far*. He drove her south on Fifth Avenue and past Central Park, but only as far as

42nd Street. Staring nervously out of the car window, Cassie wished desperately she could be out there among the lights and the hurrying crowds – even the whirling snow – if it meant she could avoid facing the Elders alone.

Alone. She shouldn't be alone.

'You have a right to a Supporter,' Ranjit had said. 'I'm not going to let you go alone . . .'

But so far, he had. He'd left her to it and she was on her own. Fine. It wouldn't be the first time she'd coped by herself. It was fine.

If only it didn't terrify her so much.

Marat had stopped the car. Cassie didn't want him to step out and open the door, she didn't want to leave the car's comforting leather-scented warmth, but there was no choice. Through the wild snow flurries and the skeletal tree branches she made out a majestic marble facade, pillared and arched and floodlit: the New York Public Library. Things were getting stranger by the minute. Marat led her between two massive marble lions, and as she nervously followed, she heard him speak for the first time.

'Patience and Fortitude,' he muttered, and gave a barking laugh she didn't like at all.

Was that what he reckoned she needed? No, she

decided: he was talking about the lions. She glanced nervously back at them. They seemed solid and almost friendly despite their size. Anyway, she'd sooner face two giant cats than what waited for her inside . . .

Wish me luck, she told them mentally, and then she was trailing Marat through the revolving doors and into a magnificent entrance hall.

The interior was spectacular. Its elegance reminded her more than anywhere else in New York of the Darke Academy in Paris – the sweeping staircases, the white marble columns, the tall arched windows, the painted ceilings. It would have taken her breath away, if she'd had any to spare. As it was, she felt small and vulnerable. Marat was enjoying her discomfort at this mystery tour, she knew it. Cassie, meanwhile, was feeling increasingly intimidated by the height of the marble ceilings and the splendid paintings of gods and mythical creatures. It didn't help that they were reminding her of her train station date with Ranjit. God, where *was* he . . . ?

Enough! she told herself. Don't worry about Ranjit! He'd be here eventually. She knew he would: he'd *promised*.

There were plenty of people milling around, but no one challenged Marat as he led her along corridors and through ranks of reading desks. No one caught her eye, not even the security guards, but she saw Marat give one of them a sly nod as he led her deeper and deeper into the library. Now there were fewer people about. Lights glowed, but in corners and passageways the shadows were thick. The warren of corridors seemed endless, as if she'd never find her way out. Cassie shivered.

Finally, Marat came to a large oak door. Without hesitating, he pushed it open and led her into a large, shadowy room, closing the heavy door behind her with a thud. It was as splendid as anywhere else in the library, panelled in dark wood and lit by sconces, but she couldn't pause to admire the ornate marble fireplace or the huge tapestries flanking it. A long and beautifully carved table faced her, with twenty or more figures seated silently behind it on gilded chairs. Candles in silver holders cast flickering light on to their shadowed faces, so that Cassie could see only flashes of feature: an ear, a sharp cheekbone, an aquiline nose. What she could see best, though, was the glint of their eyes – and every single one was fixed on her.

As her own vision adjusted to the dimness she held her breath. However obscured by shadows, some of these faces were familiar. Two strikingly beautiful women and one man were instantly recognisable film actors. There were faces that were completely unknown to her, too, but she definitely knew that high-profile entrepreneur, and that fashion designer. She even knew the female senator who'd stood in the last Presidential race. And the British cabinet minister – wasn't he in New York on a trade mission? That's what it had said in the paper . . .

They observed her wordlessly. Were they waiting for her to speak? OK, she'd played a game or two of chicken in her life, but this was pretty unnerving. A chair had been set down facing them; she didn't wait for an invitation, but sat down. Crossed her ankles. Uncrossed them again.

Studying the line of impassive faces, she did a double take as she spotted Sir Alric Darke. He gave the tiniest nod of acknowledgement, but she'd never seen him look so severe. Creepier and curiouser . . . And there was even something familiar about the ice-blonde woman who sat beside Sir Alric, directly in front of Cassie and in the centre of the table. She had blade-sharp features, and possibly the coldest eyes Cassie had ever seen. Possibly. She'd seen a similar gaze before . . .

The voice that finally broke the silence was dry, dispassionate, and terrifying.

'The Council of Elders is called to order. Brigitte Svensson presiding.'

CHAPTER TWENTY

'So, Miss Bell. Perhaps you would like to explain your recent . . . episode?'

Cassie hooked one ankle over the other again, and clasped her hands round her knees. There. That might stop them shaking. And doing that made her sit forward a bit, so that she couldn't flinch back from Katerina's mother.

It must be her. The name, the icy beauty, the hatred oozing out of every pore. Unless Katerina had aged overnight, Brigitte Svensson had to be the mother of Cassie's nemesis.

'Episode?' Cassie stalled.

'Tch! Don't waste our time. The incident at Carnegie Hall.'

Hoping for some moral support, Cassie sought out Sir Alric, but he wasn't even looking at her. He was studying one of the tapestries, as if none of this was anything to do with him. Again she felt a bitter stab of betrayal.

'I don't know what happened,' she said curtly.

'Really?' The voice held a cold undercurrent of mockery. 'Perhaps you mean you don't know what happened apart from a public loss of control, a display that endangered the very existence of the Few, and a near-fatal attack on a fellow member?' Brigitte glanced sneeringly at Sir Alric, but he didn't react. Cassie was beginning to loathe him. 'Yes, I can quite see how that might slip what passes for your mind.'

'I meant,' said Cassie through her teeth, 'I don't know *how* it happened. It wasn't intentional.'

'As I said, a complete loss of control.' Brigitte sighed, and turned to her fellow Elders. 'Our fears regarding this member have very much come to pass. You will all remember that the Bell girl was mooted as a potential host late last year. The proposal was vetoed with, as it turns out, extremely good reason. She is not and never has been Few material. Had it not been for an appalling breach of Few law, she would now be perfectly *adequate* feeding material. No more.'

The man beside Brigitte leaned forward into the light, and Cassie saw steel-blue eyes, cropped hair, a distinctive cleft in his chin. She took a silent gasp of breath, as if she'd been punched in the gut. That face: she'd only seen it for a second, but she wouldn't forget it. It was one of the FBI men who had come to the Academy to arrest Jake.

'The girl's a danger to herself,' he drawled. 'And to the rest of us.'

'She's inexperienced, Vaughan, that's all.' Someone interrupted, and Cassie glanced gratefully at the black-haired woman. 'Her initiation was irregular and she hasn't been properly trained. That's all. Give her a chance.'

I will never, thought Cassie, *never* have a bad word to say about one of your movies again.

'We could consider repeating the ceremony.' That was the cabinet minister. 'Has that ever been attempted?'

'Of course not,' snapped Vaughan. 'It's never been necessary. This is unprecedented.'

'Then I suggest we set a precedent.' The British man's frigid tone suggested there was no love lost between him and the American man.

'How?' The senator shrugged. 'Estelle Azzedine is dead and buried.'

But her spirit's alive and kicking!

Cassie jumped at Estelle's voice, but none of the Council seemed to notice. Brigitte narrowed her eyes, though.

The film actress spoke again. 'Put it this way, something went wrong. We don't know what. But really, her case is quite fascinating. Shouldn't we instead be looking to see how we can help? None of this is really Miss Bell's fault, after all.'

'That's irrelevant,' said another woman. 'Fault isn't at issue here. She's clearly dangerous. We're not here to give her group therapy so she can adjust – we need to deal with this matter swiftly and decisively.'

'Let's not be rash. Studying her . . . *ability* may well be of great significance for all of us.' Perhaps that cabinet minister felt some national allegiance.

'Whether that's true or not, we can't take the risk.'

'But you'll take the risk of punishing her? An innocent party?'

'Hardly innocent.'

'The Carnegie Hall incident was a disaster . . .'

'No, the damage limitation worked. It's been smoothed over. Donations in the right places.'

'And next time? And the next?'

'ENOUGH!'

Brigitte's cry echoed, easily drowning the quarrelling voices, and hush fell on the whole room. Cassie swallowed reflexively. Brigitte drew out the silence until the air crackled, and when she spoke again her voice was as soft and chilled as snow.

'There can be no doubting the girl is dangerous. There

can be no doubting she cannot control herself. We have responsibilities, ladies and gentlemen, not only to our fellow Few, but to the public at large. Kindly imagine the repercussions when she kills someone.' Again she left a dramatic pause for her damning words to sink in. 'She attacked a Few member, in full view of the public. She was also responsible, may I remind the Council, for an assault last term that left my own daughter brutally scarred. I propose we expel Miss Bell from the Academy . . .'

'I second Brigitte.'

Brigitte looked over at the FBI man with a hint of annoyance. 'Thank you, Vaughan, but I have a further proposal to lay before this Council: that Miss Bell, for her own protection and ours, should be incarcerated indefinitely in the Confine.'

Cassie leaped to her feet, her intake of breath splitting the horrible silence. What the hell was the Confine?

'What do you—'

'Please sit down, Miss Bell. You will not improve your situation by further demonstration of your inability to control yourself.'

'But . . .' Cassie looked desperately at the row of Elders. None would meet her eye, not even her erstwhile supporters. 'You can't put me in prison, it's not—'

'It is fair, just, and reasonable. The Confine is not a prison. Not in the way you understand the word.' Brigitte gave a loud sigh. 'Things could have been very much worse for you. Be grateful for the Council's mercy.' She raised a silver gavel. 'Now, if the Council is unanimously agreed, I hereby—'

'Wait.'

Brigitte hesitated, her gavel hovering, her face darkening with anger. Cassie felt her breath sigh out of her in a great rush, and her muscles trembled. She slumped back into her seat.

Sir Alric had spoken. At last.

'Brigitte is right in one respect. We do not know what Cassandra is capable of. None of us do, and that includes me.' Thoughtfully he turned a pen in his fingers, his unsmiling eyes meeting Cassie's. 'But may I respectfully suggest that this fact alone renders the Confine an unsuitable place to hold her.'

'But—' Vaughan had turned crimson.

Sir Alric ignored the FBI man. 'She would be best monitored in an environment where she is entirely under the supervision of experienced Few. Where her power can be measured and controlled, and if necessary turned to our advantage – rather than constrained and possibly warped against us. Where she can be taught the self-control she so clearly lacks. I propose to the Council that there is only one appropriate place to keep her.' He paused and looked at each of the council members in turn. 'At the Academy. Under my supervision and control. For the foreseeable future.'

Murmurs rose from the Elders, but Cassie could make none of them out: only that some were angry and negative, some relieved and supportive. Her head was buzzing. Could the man have left his intervention any later? On the other hand, his timing had been mighty effective . . .

But Brigitte wasn't about to give up.

'Ah, Sir Alric,' she said, her voice dripping contempt. 'Perhaps it is you who should be under supervision and control. It's your responsibility to keep Academy students in line and out of the limelight. Something you seem to have singularly failed to do in this case.'

Sir Alric smiled thinly, but Cassie could have sworn she saw sparks whirl in the depths of his eyes.

'Until what happened at Carnegie Hall, none of us had any idea that Cassandra's powers were so . . . unique. I can hardly be held responsible for failing to see a threat that escaped the wisdom of the whole Council. I have many talents, Brigitte, but the ability to predict the future is not one of them. My proposal stands.'

Brigitte's voice trembled with thwarted rage. 'There are then two proposals before the Council. We shall put them to a vote.'

Sir Alric's face was impassive as they began to vote. Cassie couldn't look at him, so she stared hard at the floor. Cowardly, maybe, but it was better than watching the expressions on the faces of the Elders, trying to count the votes for and against her. By the time Marat had gathered the voting slips and they had been counted, and recounted – then counted a third time – Cassie was dizzy with suspense and fear.

'By a majority of one . . .' Brigitte halted.

Cassie's head snapped up to stare at her. The woman's lips were tight, her teeth gritted.

'By a majority of *one*, the Council has decreed that Cassandra Bell will return to the Darke Academy.' She rapped her gavel so hard Cassie was amazed the table didn't shatter.

Marat was at her side. It was over. Getting to her feet, Cassie shot a grateful glance at Sir Alric, but once again he was ignoring her. There was nothing for it but to gather her dignity and follow Marat from the room in silence. There was no point trying to make conversation with the little brute. He looked more sullen than ever. Disappointed, maybe.

It was only as the door closed behind them that she heard Brigitte's voice rise once more, over-sweet and clipped, and, Cassie suspected, made clear enough for her to hear.

'We move on to the next item of business.' A rap of the gavel. 'The Johnson boy.'

CHAPTER TWENTY-ONE

The Johnson boy . . . ?

Cassie stopped in her tracks as Marat moved ahead of her through the reading room. The place was still in near-darkness and the shelves were high to right and left.

Jake.

Glowering ahead, it must have taken Marat a while to register that her footsteps had stopped. He was ten metres away when he finally turned.

For a moment they eyed each other warily. Marat took one step towards her.

'I need to go to the toilet!' yelped Cassie. Before Marat could react, she had turned and run into the shadows between the bookshelves. She had to get back to that room.

One thing about being Few, she thought appreciatively: it made her fast. Fast, and nimble on her feet. Her heart pounded as she switched direction and darted between the shelves.

In the deepest shadows, she paused. She could see Marat in between the stacks, searching for her. She hoped her own heartbeat wasn't as loud as it sounded.

Dodging through the bookshelves, she alternately crept and sprinted silently, retracing her steps in an elaborate circle. By the time she spotted a familiar sign to the Trustees' Room, she couldn't hear him any more. Holding her breath, she peered into every corner, but there was no further sign of Marat. Almost too easy . . .

Breathing again, heart racing, she crept back towards the Council meeting room. She was pretty certain she'd lost him, and she doubted that the porter would rush to tell the Elders that he'd let her give him the slip: what kind of problems would that make for him? Hopefully he'd bank on her making her own way back to the Academy, since she didn't have any other option.

Cassie pressed her ear to the door, grateful all over again for the Few spirit and its effect on her hearing. She could clearly make out the raised voices of the Elders, and she'd made it in time to hear their decision. Only just, but thank God she had.

'Silence for the decision!' Brigitte's voice again, coldly triumphant this time. 'By a majority of seventeen, the

Council decrees that Jake Johnson will be removed from Federal custody within the next twenty-four hours, and placed in the Confine.'

What? Cassie couldn't believe what she was hearing.

'All business being completed and no further matters arising, I declare this Council of Elders closed.' The sharp blow of that silver gavel set Cassie's teeth on edge.

Swiftly, she backed into the shadows, praying none of them would turn as they filed out. Just as well she'd had so much practice in staying unseen in darkened corridors back at Cranlake Crescent. None of the Elders noticed her pressed against the wall beyond the light of the sconces. Probably none of them ever imagined anyone would dare to eavesdrop on their fancy Council.

It made her heart sink to her stomach, seeing them up close. Besides the Elders she had already recognised, there were more. People of power, people of influence. People she'd seen on the cover of news-stand magazines. Jesus, thought Cassie. If they ever turned against her as one . . .

They'd turned against Jake. They were placing him in the Confine.

Not a prison, Brigitte had said. Not in the way *you* understand.

Oh, Cassie reckoned she understood fine.

215

Not all of them had come out of the room. At least two were missing, and they were the two who really mustn't see her. As Cassie forced herself to stay still, barely breathing, she heard Brigitte's soft, snowflake voice.

'So, Vaughan, the usual measures are in place?'

'Everything is arranged. The boy will go to the Confine immediately. As far as the Council is concerned, that will be the end of the matter.'

Cassie stopped breathing altogether. What did that mean, 'As far as the Council is concerned'?

'Good,' said Brigitte. 'And don't worry – the system is foolproof. In all the years I have been in charge of the Confine, the Elders have never once bothered to check on their guests. I've taken dozens of them. It will be years before anyone realises the boy isn't there – if they ever do.'

'They'll still be furious.' Vaughan didn't sound too worried; in fact, Cassie detected an undercurrent of laughter.

'Perhaps. But no more than I am. My daughter's attacker received a mere slap on the wrist tonight.' Brigitte's voice trembled with anger. 'If the Singh boy hadn't meddled, my daughter would have been successful in getting rid of the half-breed bitch herself, and neatly made it look like an accident to boot.'

Cassie clamped her hand over her mouth to stop the gasp. The 'accident' at Grand Central Station. That had been Katerina? And now Jake's certainty that it had been Katerina who had tried to abduct Isabella at Coney Island didn't seem so ridiculous either. Could that have been Brigitte? The pair looked similar enough to be mistaken for each other at a distance.

'You'll bring the boy to the cottage tonight as usual? It's been rather too long since the Living Soil was fed. Giving it that snitch of a boy will be some measure of vengeance for what those brats did to my Katerina.' In a silky murmur she added, 'Besides, I've been so good, Vaughan. I'm entitled to a treat . . .'

Chills rippled down Cassie's spine, so that she had to make an effort to stay absolutely still. The Living What?

The Living Soil, Cassandra!

Estelle's voice held something strange. Was that disbelief? Excitement?

Terror?

'What is it, Estelle? What's the Living Soil?' Cassie whispered.

Estelle's voice was a throaty murmur:

There are prisons far, far more evil than the Confine, my dear . . .

CHAPTER TWENTY-TWO

Cassie didn't bother with the lift. Bolting across the marble atrium of the Academy, ignoring the stares of other students, she tore off her gloves and scarf as she ran. Shoving through to the fire escape stairs, she took them two at a time. It was faster. At least, it was at the speed she could run. And she needed to run, to work off this terrible anger and fear.

Ranjit's room was on the fifth floor, but she reached it barely out of breath. That was Estelle again. She was beginning to know how much she relied on Estelle. How much she needed and appreciated that powerful presence.

She didn't bother to knock. When she burst in, Ranjit was just pulling off his shirt and the shower was running. In nothing but his designer jeans, he stared at her dumbfounded. His smile, when it came, was forced, trying to cover something else.

'Well. This is unexpected but nice—' He stopped short as soon as he saw Cassie's furious expression.

She took a ragged breath. 'What happened to you?'

'Your Council meeting. I know it was tonight—'

'So where were you, Ranjit? I waited for you!'

Screwing his expensive shirt into a ball, he twisted it between his fingers. His gaze darted over her shoulder at the door, then back to her. 'There was . . . Something came up – something that meant I couldn't come, Cassie. I wanted to tell you, honestly I did, but if—'

'Not good enough!' She was too angry to cry. 'You *promised*. You said you'd be there!'

'And I wanted to, more than anything. Please, Cassie, you have to believe me. But I—'

'I don't want to hear it. I don't want to hear what was more important, OK? I just want you to know,' – she swallowed hard – 'that you might not have seen me again.'

Ranjit sank down on to the bed, shoving his hair out of his eyes as he stared up at her. The room was filling with steam, but he didn't move to turn off the shower. When he spoke, his voice was shaky. 'What happened?'

'*Ms* Brigitte Svensson was in the chair,' spat Cassie. 'And I avoided the Confine by one vote.'

'Cassie. Oh, God, Cassie. I didn't know it was her. I wasn't told . . . Listen—'

'No! I don't want to listen. You left me to face that *alone*. So now, you owe me some answers, Ranjit. The Confine – what is it?'

'The Confine . . .' He stood up, pacing the room. She couldn't help watching, her gaze drawn to his damp, naked torso. Yesterday she'd have been leaping on him like a tiger. Yesterday she'd have eaten him alive, in a good way.

But now she felt numbed by the leaden weight in her chest. 'The Confine, Ranjit.'

He half-glanced at her. 'Didn't they tell you?'

'It sounded like a prison to me, but apparently my feeble understanding of a prison is not what this Confine is. So maybe you can explain it?'

'It's – listen, you don't have to go there, right? Just try and put it out of your mind.'

'*I* don't have to go!' she yelled, tears stinging her eyes. 'But Jake does!'

'Jake?' Ranjit scraped his hands through his black hair, damp from the steam.

'Yes, Jake! He's been sentenced to the Confine. I heard them! I doubled back after they sent me out and I heard them!'

'You eavesdropped? On the *Council*?'

'You bet your bloody life I eavesdropped!' She sighed. 'Ranjit, you have to help me now. What are we going to do?'

Swiftly, as if making a decision, he seized her arms and gazed into her eyes. 'Nothing. We're going to do nothing, Cassie. We can't go against the Council.'

For a fraction of a second she was stupefied. 'What?'

'Listen to me. What the Council told you was true – the Confine isn't like a prison, it's more like a . . . a luxury hotel. It's where the Elders keep people who know too much about the Few and can't be trusted to keep quiet. Jake won't be a prisoner. He'll be a guest, Cassie, a guest of the Few.'

She stared at him, unable to believe her ears. 'A guest for *ever*? A guest who can't choose to leave?'

'Well, yes, but—'

'That is a *prisoner*, Ranjit!'

Lost for words, she slumped on to the bed. Hesitantly he moved beside her, stroking her cheek. His fingers trembled, as if he was reluctant to touch her but couldn't help himself. Despite the steam, she shivered.

'Cassie, there's nothing we can do. I'm sorry.'

She couldn't look at his face so instead she focused again on his lean, muscled chest. It meant nothing; she felt nothing. Must be shock.

Quietly she said, 'I haven't told you the worst.'

'What? What else could there be?'

'Brigitte. And a man called Vaughan. He's FBI – Isabella and I saw him taking Jake away – but he's also Few. One of the Elders. They're planning to double-cross the Council.'

Ranjit laughed. 'I'd like to see them try.'

'You damn well will, then! They've done it before! What Brigitte is planning for Jake – I overheard that too. They have a whole system in place. It sounds horrible, Ranjit. Horrible. She takes people from the Confine to something called the Living Soil.'

Ranjit sucked in a breath, and his face paled. Then he shook his head violently. 'No. No way, Cassie. You misheard.'

'I did not!'

'Then she was bluffing! Showing off! Posturing! It isn't going to happen, Cassie. Please, you have to trust me.'

His eyes were pleading. She opened her mouth to say, Of course I do! But the words wouldn't come. Instead, she broke his stare. 'I don't care if you don't believe me. She's definitely got something planned for Jake and it isn't the Confine. We've got to—'

'No! No, Cassie, listen. You mustn't get involved in this. Seriously, I'm really frightened for you.' He put a warm arm around her. 'Brigitte will not do anything to Jake, not against the Council's wishes. But she is hugely powerful. It's you she'll target.'

'She already did! Or Katerina did anyway. Grand Central? It was her who tried to push me on to the tracks.'

'What?'

'Forget it. Look, Ranjit, we just need to help Jake. Please. If we get him out of the Confine then maybe—'

'You can't interfere with Council business, Cassie.'

'No, but *you* can! Ranjit, I've seen the way they look at you here – the other Few, even Sir Alric. You're powerful, you must have some influence.'

'No. No, Cassie, I can't. The Council's decision is final. None of us can go against them.'

She couldn't believe what she was hearing. 'You could *try*!'

'Maybe I could, but I won't. Jake *is* a danger to us. He knows too much. He could expose us at any time. Get the Academy shut down. I don't want any part of that.' He turned aside so she couldn't see his eyes. 'I don't want that any more than the Council does.'

Ranjit's words took a second or two to sink into her brain, burning like hot lead. Then, with a deep, ragged breath, she tore his arm from her shoulder, pushed him away and stood up.

'That's it, isn't it? It's Jake. You *want* to get rid of him. That's what this is!'

'No. No, that's not it.'

'Yes! From the way you're acting, I wouldn't be surprised if it was you that tipped off the FBI about those files – led your buddy Vaughan right to him!'

'Come on. Be realistic, Cassie!' Ranjit snapped, rising to his feet to face her. 'What do you know? You are newly Few, or part-Few at least! You're one of us now. Do you have you any idea what would happen if the Academy were to close? The Academy is the Few's deal with the world. It's how the spirits find new hosts! It's how we teach those hosts control! Without the Academy, the Few will descend into chaos and random killing. Is that what you want, Cassie? If Jake destroys the Academy, he won't destroy the Few. He'll unleash them on the world, unchecked. He'll destroy more lives than you can count!'

The blood had drained from her face. She felt as if she was truly seeing him for the first time. '*You* destroy lives! *We* destroy them! It isn't Jake, it's the *Few*. Why should Jake, or anyone innocent, be punished for our existence?'

'Because there *is* no punishment for the Few!' he roared. 'How do you punish an immortal spirit? How? I'm sorry about Jake, but there's nothing I can do. He's unlucky, that's all!'

'Like his sister was?' hissed Cassie.

'Don't you dare bring that up again, Cassie. Don't you damn well dare!' Ranjit's expression twisted viciously, his eyes narrowing. 'In fact, I'll *tell* you how to punish an immortal spirit. By splitting it! Leaving half of it in some disgusting *void*!'

The silence between them was electric. Cassie could hear her own heart thrashing, and she was sure she could hear his. On his shoulder, she could see the familiar markings of the Few begin to smoulder red.

'How dare you!' she screamed.

I am split! Divided! He UNDERSTANDS! I told you, my *dear, he's the one for us! Grab him, take him . . .*

'Estelle!'

The power surged through her so hard she almost stumbled, as if Estelle had physically thrown her towards Ranjit. When she jerked up her head, her lips were drawn back from her teeth and the world was tinged with scarlet.

Ranjit was crouched, as if he was ready to defend himself. But he was straining towards her, too, about to attack. No, not attack. Just to leap on her, seize her, own her . . .

His irises glowed vermillion. As the colour deepened to scarlet, it spread across the whites of his eyes. The colour, seen through her own red mist, was the most intense red she could imagine. He let out a starving, longing snarl.

'NO!'

Ranjit put his hands to his face, clenched into fists. His whole body shook, as if with a fever, but somehow, *somehow* he regained control. When he brought his hands down, his eyes were no longer glowing red.

They stood for a long moment, shaking, both of them gasping for breath. When Ranjit spoke again, his voice was barely above a whisper, almost as though he was talking to himself.

'This was such a goddamn mistake. Such a stupid, stupid thing to do. I should have known better.'

'Better than what?' She was dazed, off balance.

Ranjit looked up at her. 'I shouldn't have done it. I should never have got involved with you, Jess!'

She reeled back as if he'd struck her.

Oh.

God.

His face was immediately stricken, realising his mistake. Almost as stricken as hers must be. When he reached out a hand, she slapped it away.

'Cassie—'

'You won't help me,' she said in a voice that didn't belong to her. 'You don't even know who I am.'

'Cassie. I'm so sorry, I—'

'I'll handle this myself. I always have. Goodbye, Ranjit.'

She turned and stormed from the room, but he caught the door before it could slam. She heard his voice ringing after her as she ran down the corridor, but it might as well have been the sound of a barking dog.

'Please! I'm sorry! Don't get involved, Cassie! Leave it! PLEASE!'

CHAPTER TWENTY-THREE

She could barely see straight. Must be something blurring her eyes, and she couldn't stop to rub it away. She had to keep running or she'd disintegrate.

'Cassie, whoah!'

She cannoned into an obstruction. Large, solid, warm. A human being. Books clattered to the floor and arms went round her, just to stop her crashing to the ground too.

'Bloody hell, Cassie Bell.'

'Richard! Let me go!'

'Like hell I will. I might be killed in the stampede.'

She tugged her arms out of his grip. 'Get lost.'

'Cassie, what's wrong?'

'Like you care. Get out of the way, or so help me I'll—'

'Look, Cassie, about the other night, when you saw me outside—'

'I said *get off*!' She flung his hands away, and rubbed her face fiercely, trying to fight back the tears. Great. The one time she could do with being angry, not upset . . .

'Cassie, come on, tell me what happened. I . . . I know you had the Council meeting.'

Cassie gave an incredulous laugh. 'What, tell Katerina's puppy dog my problems? So you can run off and tell her ladyship?'

'Cassie, my angel,' he said smoothly, looking not the least bit shamefaced, 'I'm friends with everyone and I talk to everyone. You've seen how weak I am in comparison to the others. It's a survival strategy. I'm not going to apologise for it.'

'How bloody diplomatic of you.' She sniffed furiously, trying to move around him. He wouldn't budge.

'Have my handkerchief.' He produced it with a flourish: Hermes, of course. She'd have been reluctant to use it, but then he added with a wink, 'Don't for God's sake wipe your nose on your sleeve, scholarship girl.'

She blew her nose pointedly into the silk.

'What's going on, Cassie?'

'Look, I need to go, OK? I'm not here to fuel your gossip machine. Thanks.' She shoved the ruined hankie back into his hands.

'Hey.' There was something very different in his voice. 'Is it Jake?'

He sounded uncharacteristically . . . serious. Hesitating, she turned on her heel, frowning slightly. 'Yes.' Slowly she walked back to him, suspicious. 'Yeah. It's Jake. What do you know about that?'

'I know he was arrested. Everybody does.' He hesitated, and lowered his voice. 'Katerina set him up, you know. She and her mother. She told me. They fed him a trail of crumbs until he'd incriminated himself so far that they could get him arrested. He'll go to the Confine, of course, but Sir Alric won't be fooled for long. He'll get Jake out, you see if he doesn't.'

Cassie sneered. 'For someone who talks to everybody, you have a piss-poor idea of what's really happening.'

'What do you mean?' For the first time Richard looked uncomfortable. 'You don't think he's going to the Confine?'

'I know he isn't.'

'What did you hear?'

'I'm not having this conversation any more.'

'Cassie!' Richard's voice was deadly earnest. 'What was it?'

She wheeled on him, exasperated. 'The Living Soil. OK? Katerina's mother is taking him to some cottage where she can feed him to the Living Soil.'

She turned away, but in a flash he was in front of her again, gripping her arm. His face was deathly white.

'Are you sure?' he whispered, horrified. 'That's . . . Katerina never mentioned that. Cassie, I'm so sorry, Look, if it's true, I think I might know—'

Suddenly he broke off and stiffened, then gave her a beatific smile.

'Well listen, darling, next time you and the Rajah have a fight, you know where I am,' he said loudly.

'What?' Cassie gaped. 'Come on, Richard, what were you going to say?'

'Oh, now that would be telling.' His old nonchalance was back, but there was something new behind it. Cassie looked around. At the end of the corridor stood Sara and another Few girl. They were eyeing her and Richard closely.

'If you know what's going on, Richard, please tell me,' she mumbled through gritted teeth.

'Hmm . . . I can be bought, but I'm *terribly* expensive.'

She stared into his eyes but they were shuttered now, guarded. What was it with him? One minute he wanted to help her – out of guilt, probably – the next he was his impenetrable, flippant self, saving face in front of those Few bitches.

Fear, perhaps. Covering his arse, more like.

He knew something – she was certain of it. But he wasn't going to tell, and she didn't have time to get into some bidding war. Making a dismissive gesture, she walked away.

'Cassie?' he called after her.

'What?' she snapped, turning. 'Don't waste my time, Richard. I don't have any.'

'This one's yours.' He thrust a book into her hands and walked away.

Taken aback despite her turmoil, she started to shout after him. 'I never dropped a—'

Too late. He was already gone.

'Isabella, we don't have much time. Come on, we have to find where they're taking Jake.'

'But I thought he was in custody with—'

'Come on!' Cassie shoved Richard's book into her bag – she could return it to him later – then grabbed Isabella's arm in one hand, her cashmere coat in the other, and pushed the two together. 'It's worse than we thought.'

Isabella fumbled her arm into the coat sleeve, her voice trembling. 'Omigod, Cassie. What is it?'

'It's going to be all right,' said Cassie, 'we just have to find Jake as soon as possible. Come on, we need to go.'

'Cassie – stop. Stop!' Isabella wound her scarf around her neck and grabbed her phone and her money from the nightstand. 'You're not making any sense!'

'You're right,' Cassie admitted. 'But I need to think, and I can't think straight in this place. Let's get out of here.'

'OK, OK, let's go. Then you can tell me everything.'

Cassie breathed a silent prayer of gratitude for Isabella's practicality as they hurried down the fire stairs. Isabella didn't know what Cassie was on about, but she didn't waste time asking. She took Cassie on trust. God, that felt good. Especially after Ranjit's betrayal . . . Cassie gave a shudder, but shook it off.

'Soon as we're out of this building we can start to plan. I just don't want to be anywhere near the Few. There's none of them I can trust.'

'What about Ran—'

'*None* of them.'

Outside on the streets, breathing in the frosty air, Cassie felt a wave of relief. Thank heavens. She'd thought she was going to suffocate.

'Right, come on, Cassie. Give!' Isabella panted as they strode briskly away from the Academy. 'Something's really wrong. You have to tell me.'

It didn't take long to give her a résumé of the Council meeting. Isabella listened in silence, but Cassie could almost feel her fuming. When she reached the part about Jake's sentence, Isabella gasped.

'But they . . . it's obscene! They can't just imprison someone for life – it's not possible.'

'It is,' Cassie told her grimly. 'But listen, even that isn't bad enough for Brigitte. She's got something else planned, Isabella. Something worse, something the Council don't know about.'

'What?'

'I wish I knew.' She rubbed her cold face with her gloved hands. 'But it's got something to do with a cottage and something called the Living Soil.'

Isabella blanched. 'That sounds . . . Cassie, that sounds bad.'

'Yes. And I've a feeling Richard knows something about it.'

'Richard?' Isabella's breath plumed in the air. 'Tell me.'

'I can't, *he* wouldn't tell *me*. One second he was talking properly, the next he'd pulled back into his shell like a little crab.'

'What did Richard say?' Isabella stared across the road, into the shadows of Central Park.

'Nothing. I told you.'

'Richard often sounds like he's talking about nothing.' Isabella had a steely, thoughtful look in her eyes, and she seemed uncharacteristically rational. 'But he *always* knows more than he lets on.'

Cassie gave a deep sigh. It all seemed suddenly, impossibly difficult. If only bloody Ranjit had come good, how different this all could have been. 'I told you. He clammed up, so I walked off. Oh, and then he shoved a book at me, even though it was him that dropped it, and before I could give it back he ran away.'

'He – ah!' Isabella clapped her hands. 'That's it. That's it! Where's the book?'

'Here.' Cassie patted her bag. 'But I told you it isn't mine, it—'

'Ye of little faith!' Isabella snatched the book from Cassie's hand as she drew it out. It was an old guidebook to New York City. Riffling through, Isabella gave a sharp cry of triumph and brandished the volume in her friend's face. The page where she'd opened it was folded down at the corner.

'Cassie! Don't you see? Richard told you where they're taking Jake!'

CHAPTER TWENTY-FOUR

'A weapon. We'll need some kind of a weapon.' Cassie pulled Isabella back towards the Academy. 'Something that we know works against the Few.'

'Uh-oh. You're not thinking about . . . Keiko's knife?'

'Yes, I am.'

Good girl! It's exactly what you need, you'll see!

Glancing at Isabella, Cassie decided against letting on that the demon in her head was giving her tips on strategy. The strange knife that they'd managed to turn on the homicidal Few girl had seemed to take care of Keiko quite efficiently last term. Jake had taken the knife after he and Isabella had rescued her at the Arc. Cassie wasn't sure quite what significance the strange weapon had, but from Estelle's agitated reaction, she figured there must be something powerful about it. And they'd need all the help they could get.

Yes! Find it, Cassandra. Find it!

Yes, yes. Shut up, Estelle.

Heh! You'll be needing me soon.

Isabella was shaking her head. 'But you don't even know where . . .'

'It's in Jake's room,' said Cassie decisively. 'If he managed to hide it before Vaughan took him, it should still be in there somewhere.'

They rushed back into the lobby of the Academy, and Cassie jabbed furiously at the call button for the lift, which seemed to take forever to arrive. When the doors at last slid open on the third floor, the place was quiet. Breathing out a sigh of relief, Cassie edged into the corridor. 'C'mon, there's no one around.'

Isabella followed her cautiously. 'You think the knife will still be in there even? The police sealed off the room after he was taken away.'

'Seals are for breaking.' Cassie pushed aside the police tape strung across Jake's door and tried the handle. 'Gimme your hair clasp.'

'How do you . . . all right.' Shrugging, Isabella slipped a silver pin from her hair and watched as Cassie slid it into the lock.

'C'mon, c'mon . . .' Cassie jiggled her improvised lockpick impatiently.

'Someone's coming!'

Cassie hissed a curse. She'd been so focused on the lock, she hadn't heard the approaching footsteps. Now she realised she'd recognise the stealthy footfalls anywhere – Marat.

There was nowhere to go. Cassie hesitated for a moment, then Isabella seized her hand and pulled her further down the corridor. Imperiously she rapped on another teak door.

As Marat's footsteps came closer, Isabella muttered something under her breath in Spanish, but her face lit in a huge smile as the door was flung open.

'Perry! Angel!' Before the startled American could slam it in her face, she had stepped neatly over the threshold, pulling Cassie with her. 'Here we are!'

Cassie started for a moment – Perry Hutton was Richard's roommate. She glanced around but there was no sight of him. She instead smiled sweetly at the loathsome Perry.

'What the— Now, look, Isabella . . .'

'Did I get the wrong date?'

'There isn't a date! What the hell are you on about? You're not my type, sweetie. And what's *she* doing here?'

Isabella maintained her smile, but her voice developed an edge as she pulled the door shut behind them. 'Be quiet, Perry. We'll be out of here in a second.'

'You'll be out of here now!'

'Throwing out one of the Few? Oh Perry, darling, you are so *brave*!'

That shut him up. Perry's eyes flickered uneasily in Cassie's direction. 'Sure, Isabella. Whatever.'

Cassie pressed her ear to the door. The footsteps had paused, for a little too long, but now they were shuffling away again towards the elevators at the end of the corridor.

'Look, can you go? Please?' Perry was turning fractious. 'I'm expecting a friend.'

Cassie leaned close to the door again, and she heard a faint but distinct *ping*, and then the muted hiss of the elevator doors. She took Isabella's arm.

'Let's go. Good luck with your *friend*, Peregrine.'

He went purple above the collar and opened his mouth, but the girls were already outside and Isabella had shut the door firmly in his bemused and angry face.

Isabella giggled. 'Pompous ass.'

'You got that one right. Quick, Marat's gone.'

Cassie slid the hairpin back into the lock. One decisive twist and the door swung open.

'Goodness. That was a piece of pie.'

'Cake. Well, I've done it before.' As Cassie ducked

under the tape and closed the door, though, she found her heart was thrashing with fear. She couldn't shake off the worry that Marat might come back and find them. That guy was like a fungus – he popped up everywhere you didn't want him.

Jake's room was neat and tidy. If Vaughan and his FBI buddy had searched the place, they'd been pretty careful. But Cassie didn't think they had – they had been more interested in getting Jake out of the Academy and into the Confine. Hastily, Cassie ran the flat of her hand between the mattress and the base of the bed, and then began to hunt behind the desk, the nightstand, the headboard.

Isabella was searching frantically too, pulling books out of a shelf, rummaging in drawers. 'I don't know where to start. If it's here, Jake must have hidden it really well. Horrible thing.'

Too well. Find it, Cassandra! Find it!

'I'm trying,' she muttered. Yanking a drawer out of Jake's desk, she upturned it, and pens and paperclips and notebooks scattered to the floor. No knife.

FIND IT!

Estelle was getting really agitated. Standing stock-still, Cassie clenched her fists and gritted her teeth. She could feel the bubbling energy, the burning that rose from the base of her spine to her blazing eyes and out. No! No, she mustn't . . .

Where is it, Cassandra? WHERE IS IT?

'Oh my God.' Isabella was gaping at her, but Cassie's attention was on the mirror on the wall beside the wardrobe. Something was drawing her to it . . .

Through a red filter Cassie stared at the mirror, and the shimmering aura that was building around her reached out to touch it. The frame was heavy, solid steel, but it began to melt in front of her eyes. The frame warped and buckled, while the silvered glass ran like treacle, sliding down inside the frame until both girls were suddenly twisted versions of themselves in its reflection.

Cassie clamped her hands to her face in horror, desperately blinking the red film away from her eyes. She took a breath, then ran to the mirror, running her hands across the melted frame, the distorted glass, her own warped reflection. Beneath her fingertips the glass surface seemed to tremble. Frowning, she tugged the mirror out from the wall and slid her fingers round the back of the frame. Something was resting precariously on the back ridge of the frame, and as her fingertips touched it, it clattered to the floor.

'Here it is,' she whispered. She lifted the knife, gazing at its elaborately carved hilt.

'OK.' Isabella's mouth twisted with distaste as she eyed the brutal knife. 'What just happened?'

Cassie looked up momentarily from the blade. 'Do ... do you mind if we don't talk about it?' Gently, she stroked the twisted figures with her thumb: the mermaids, the caryatids, something half-cat, half-snake. She could have sworn they responded to her touch, stirred and stretched . . . It felt almost as if it belonged in her hand, against her skin, and somewhere in her head she heard Estelle give a shuddering sigh of pleasure.

Isn't it beautiful?

Cassie shivered and tucked the knife inside her coat.

'I don't like that thing,' said Isabella.

Mildly irritated, Cassie avoided Isabella's gaze. 'We need it.'

'But could you use it?'

Cassie didn't answer.

The air outside was electric with an impending storm: Cassie could taste the charge in the air, feel the tips of her hair lifting. As they dodged the traffic and made their way to the 79th Street entrance of Central Park, she could feel the knife inside her coat, warm against her body. Isabella was right – was she really ready for this? Could she actually use the knife, if it came to it?

'This way, Cassie!' Isabella's hushed voice was fraught with anxiety.

Cassie shook her head free of doubts and ran on after her friend into the shadows and through pools of streetlight on the 79th Street Transverse. She knew this path: she'd walked it in the daylight, that time two weeks ago when she'd gone skating at the Wollman Rink with Ranj—

Not now, she thought, shoving him out of her head.

She convinced herself she wasn't scared going into the darkness under the East Drive bridge – why should she be? she thought – and on the other side she saw a suggestion of water. A distant flash of lightning made the Turtle Pond gleam like a mirror for an instant, then darkness closed in again. She could feel cold rain on her face, but as the wind rose it didn't slow her. Isabella was out of breath, lagging behind her now, but Cassie felt she could run for ever.

'How much further?' she barked.

'Right there!' Stumbling to a halt, Isabella grabbed her. 'That's it – the Swedish Cottage. It's a puppet theatre.'

An American flag and a Swedish one hung on the roof of the large wooden building, wet and whipped by gusts of wind.

Cassie let out a mirthless laugh. She should have

realised Brigitte wouldn't have been taking Jake to one of her own properties. Besides, she couldn't imagine Katerina's family owning anything smaller than a mansion.

Cassie felt her muscles tense as she prowled closer through the trees. 'Looks quiet,' she murmured.

It was raining in earnest now, the drops stinging like ice on her skin. The building itself wasn't lit, but she could make out a faint glow from behind it. She narrowed her eyes, silenced her breathing. Behind the rising wind and the roar of the rain, she could hear something.

Voices. Movements. The scrape of a shovel blade on soil. Low laughter.

Lightning exploded directly above them, turning the world white. In the fraction of a second before the thunder shook the earth, Cassie saw what was happening: saw the figures and what they were doing, frozen in the light like a tableau.

The lightning bolt was followed instantly by a second flash. Cassie was aware of a distorted, inhuman form rising up before her. Flinching reflexively, she stumbled back.

Then it was right in front of her, a hideous face screaming into hers, its eyes burning red with hate and power.

There was no time to react. Lifted off her feet by a

ringing blow, Cassie felt herself flung through the electric air, her skull thudding hard on to the solid earth as she landed. Struggling to right herself, another lightning bolt flashed through the night without warning and crashed into a nearby tree. Cassie had a moment of clarity as she saw the branch rip off like a disused limb and hurtle towards her. And then the night went truly black.

CHAPTER TWENTY-FIVE

Consciousness returned like a cold slap. Trying to get to her feet, Cassie felt the heavy tree branch pinning her to the ground. Mustering all her strength, she managed to heave it off, but felt a searing, piercing pain as she took a breath. At least one rib was broken. She coughed and gasped again as pain shot through her once more. Around her the rain howled; lightning, more distant now, crackled across the skyline.

'Silly girl. Silly, stupid scholarship girl, to think you were a match for us, even with your freaky powers. And greedy old Mother Nature had to take her turn too. That lightning bolt nearly lit you up like a Christmas tree.'

She didn't recognise the expensive black boots, but she knew the voice.

Katerina.

Desperately, Cassie lashed out with a fist, but the feet

in front of her skipped lightly back. The Swedish girl's evasive manoeuvre revealed silhouettes behind her. They looked human and yet . . . not. There was something distorted about the figures: as distorted as Katerina's grotesque form. Oh, Cassie recognised that, all right. She'd seen it before, at the Arc de Triomphe – Katerina, letting her true evil Few colours shine through. The peeled-back lips, the red eyes, the teeth that weren't down to any all-American orthodontist . . .

The girl was still stylish, though. Chic, despite the casual ease with which she held Isabella's unconscious form, tucked under one sinewy arm.

'Gods, you three have the luck of the devil,' Katerina laughed. 'I've tried and I've tried to get my revenge a little more elegantly, but it all comes down to fisticuffs and flying tree branches in the end.'

'Isabella!' Cassie reached for her friend. 'Don't hurt her!'

'Don't worry about your roomie, dear. I'll take care of her.' The grey lips stretched further. 'Once and for all.'

With a snarl of rage, Cassie tried to lunge up and snatch at Isabella, but Katerina dodged her with laughable ease. One of those expensively shod feet lashed out, catching Cassie's temple and sending her reeling back.

Damn it, if only she could focus, work through this pain . . . Cassie blinked hard, shaking her dizzy head. She was sure she knew those two figures behind Katerina; she'd seen them so recently. Lurching forwards again, still incapable of standing upright, she squinted into the driving rain and the dancing shadows. Contemptuously, Katerina turned her back on Cassie and stalked towards her comrades with Isabella hanging like a rag doll in her arms.

As Cassie crawled desperately forward, digging her fingers into the muddy grass, blinking rain out of her eyes, she saw the figures in the distance more clearly. The taller one had pale platinum hair, trimmed shorter than Katerina's but otherwise the same. The other was a broad, muscular figure, crop-haired and thick-lipped, his eyes pale and cruel. Those features were all that distinguished them from a nightmare. But she definitely knew them.

Brigitte and Vaughan, her tormentors from the Council.

Each bore a fiercely burning firebrand that didn't so much as gutter, despite the howl of the wind and the lashing rain. Dizzy, able only to gape in horror, Cassie watched the flames flicker and leap. They looked alive: squirming, jumping with life. She saw eyes, tails, wings, fangs . . . wriggling creatures in the flames. Their blazing shapes swirled amidst the darkness, illuminating another form, barely moving, lying on the sodden ground.

Jake!

With an angry cry of despair Cassie dragged herself forward. She didn't care about Brigitte and Vaughan; she didn't even care about Katerina. She needed to get to her friends.

Cassie opened her mouth to shout their names, but a whimper of pain was all that escaped her lips. She stared, helpless, as Brigitte lashed her foot into Jake's side and he stifled a groan. Cassie tried again to move, but there was no strength in her limbs.

Katerina dumped her burden beside Jake. Isabella was limp as death.

'There's a tear in my eye,' the Swedish girl rasped. 'Sweet of the lovely Sara to let me know you were coming, girls. And lucky too – Richard was supposed to be keeping an eye on you all for me, but he seems to have changed sides. I'll have to deal with him later. Still, maybe it hasn't worked out too badly. Now you Three Musketeers can be all for one.' She threw a scornful glance over at Cassie and gave a merciless laugh.

'Touching, ain't it,' growled the warped Vaughan, grinning like a skull. Cassie saw his white teeth flash in the lightning.

'Yes, well we can't separate these two lovebirds,' cooed Katerina, gazing down at Isabella and Jake. 'Don't worry, darlings, *you'll* be fed to the earth together. Unfortunately, your little half-breed friend will have to make do with a good old-fashioned killing. We can't have whatever bit of her can claim to be Few corrupting the Living Soil now, can we?'

With one foot, Katerina rolled Jake's body another metre along the ground, and Brigitte and Vaughan lifted their flaming torches high. The leaping light caught the edge of a shadow that was deeper than any of the others.

'Oh God,' whispered Cassie.

Jake lay on the lip of a black gouge in the earth. There was something strange about the pit, something evil. Cassie crawled closer. The damp earth inside it had a crimson shade, a glow. Blood red. She blinked the driving rain out of her eyes.

Cassandra, what did I tell you?

'What, Estelle?' Cassie's voice was no more than a croak, drowned by the clatter of the rain. 'What did you tell me? Should I have listened, you old bitch?'

Of course you should, dear girl. There was a strange sorrow in Estelle's voice along with the irrepressible thrill. *The Living Soil, my dear. The cruellest prison of all. Centuries of burials, feeding it, feeding those who dare to draw its power . . .*

Now she could see, but all she wanted to do was look away. *Run* away. The earth in the pit wasn't just earth – there were bodies in there too, tangled together, moving and churning, too many to count. Limbs, torsos, straggling blood-soaked hair. As the twisted pile turned, a hand clawed hopelessly at the air. Then, with a muffled scream, it was dragged under once more.

'They're not dead,' whispered Cassie, as pain thundered in her skull and her body shook. She felt sick. 'They're not dead!'

Yes, my dear. Yes. Now you understand.

And she did.

Isabella and Jake were going to be buried alive.

CHAPTER TWENTY-SIX

'An expensive schooling is all very well.' There was cruel laughter in Brigitte's voice as she raised her torch. 'But there's such a thing, dear Miss Caruso, as Too Much Information. And you have it.' She spat on Isabella's prostrate body.

'And then of course there's Jake,' smiled Katerina. 'Poor, nosy little Scooby. Don't you know curiosity killed the cretin?'

Jake ignored her, his arms encircling Isabella protectively.

'He'll soon have plenty of time to ponder all those precious files he worked so hard to dig up,' snarled Vaughan. 'Did you really think you managed to hack the FBI site on your own? We just needed an excuse to nab you, punk. Too easy. We fed you those files, just like we're gonna feed you to the Soil. Wanna call your lawyer again, sonny?' His lip curled into a mocking sneer.

Jake's voice was a low, determined growl. 'You're gonna get hell from your Council, you sick bastards. And when they find out what you've done, they'll do my job for me.' He stared up at Katrina, hatred burning in his eyes. 'You *will* pay for killing my sister.'

'We must begin,' Brigitte growled with a feverish urgency. 'Ignore the boy. What the Council doesn't know can't hurt their delicate sensibilities.'

She seized Isabella's hair, wrapping it round her gnarled, grey fingers and dragging her to the lip of the hole. Seizing him in a headlock, Vaughan hauled the choking Jake after her.

With her free hand, Brigitte reached over the pit, moaning as the red glow caressed her skin.

'The power! Oh gods, I feel it already!'

Katerina and Vaughan looked on, their breath rasping with excitement.

'The dead of centuries . . . Feel them, daughter! Feel their energy! Fed to the Soil, preserved forever, alive forever, for *us*!' Her voice rose to a hysterical, throbbing cry. 'We are the *true* Few! There is no weakness in us, no taint of mercy. We alone have the strength to feed the Living Soil, and feed *from* it. Feel its power! How could the Council have renounced it? HOW?'

Brigitte reeled as she shoved Jake to the brink of the pit, dizzy with anticipation. 'Fetch the half-breed,' she hissed, still staring mesmerised at the gouged earth. 'We'll deal with her next.'

Cassie was unable to move.

If you want to stop this, darling girl, you're running out of time . . .

What can I do?

Use the Soil, Cassandra. Turn their own power against them! The energy is all there – there in the Soil itself. You just have to reach out and take it!

It wasn't a conscious decision. It wasn't a real thought at all. At Estelle's prompt, Cassie took a deep breath and, ignoring the spike of pain that brought, simply closed her eyes and let the rage take over.

Her drained helplessness was forgotten, her exhaustion swamped by the force that zinged, blistering hot, through her veins and sinews as she drew the energy from the Soil through the air and into her lungs. It was more powerful than any feeding, more powerful than the Tears, even. Surprise barely registered as she felt her damaged rib begin to heal. The darkness turned vermillion and, swifter and stronger than before, the Cassie of Carnegie Hall was back. With a howling roar, she leaped to her feet.

'STOP!'

The three monsters turned on her, momentarily stunned.

'Oh, don't you ever *learn*?' Katerina gave a vicious snarl, but it was Vaughan who sprang at her first.

Poor, pitiful fool!

Cassie laughed, tightening her fists at her sides. She hadn't moved an inch towards his flying form, when she felt the power rip through her and then out and *beyond* her, hammering into Vaughan, stopping him in his tracks.

YES! Show him! HE ASKED FOR IT!

Distantly she heard Vaughan's howl of pain and terror. He was still metres away, scrabbling at his neck, trying to loosen her invisible stranglehold.

No use.

She smiled. He was screeching hoarsely, wasting what breath he could get. Baring her teeth, she forced him back. His feet and legs kicked and flailed at the ground but he couldn't stop her driving him back, and back, to the lip of the pit. Then, lifting him into the air, Cassie flung him backwards into the squirming, nightmarish open grave.

Vaughan let out a bellowing scream, groping at the lip of the ragged hole, trying to scramble back up the red earth walls. But he couldn't keep his footing, not in that roiling maelstrom of living corpses. As he stumbled, blood-soaked hands reached up for him, clutching his legs, his arms, his neck. For long seconds, Cassie watched as he struggled, his screams growing softer and more muffled as he was swallowed by the pit of flesh.

But then came a rumbling, like an earthquake deep underground. The gaping hole began to shift, the bloody mire bubbling violently. It seemed that Vaughan's entry was unwelcome . . .

'NO!' Brigitte's scream pierced the night. 'He'll destroy it!'

She flung herself at the open earth, reaching wildly for Vaughan's hand, clutching vainly at the air. But it was too late. He was gone. And with a shudder, the gouged earth folded on itself, knitting together like a scar. Both Brigitte and Katerina were hunched on the ground, aghast.

For Cassie, however, it was as if a plug had been pulled. The power was gushing out of her. Suddenly, inexplicably weak, she fell forward on to her knees.

The Soil!

'Estelle . . . ?' Cassie murmured, barely able to speak. 'What's . . . happening?'

You've ruined it, my dear. It cannot hold one of the Few without such disastrous results. It's gone. The Soil and its energy are gone.

Bad timing.

As one, the mother-and-daughter team turned and flung themselves towards Cassie, screaming with fury, pale platinum hair bristling with the static of the storm.

How weak you are. Dear, darling Cassandra . . .

'God, Estelle. Help me.'

Oh Cassandra. You do have another option, of course. If only you'd allow it . . .

'I can't move,' she gasped. 'Estelle . . .'

How much do you want it, darling? To live, how much? Will you allow it? I'd so love it if you did . . . I don't want us to die . . .

Hot tears coursed down Cassie's cheeks, trickling into her mouth. She tried to stand but she didn't have the energy. She could only crouch, waiting for them to tear her apart. She didn't have the strength to do this on her own.

'Please, Estelle! HELP ME!'

It's so simple, darling. It always has been. Just let it in. The rest of me. LET IT IN!

It was louder than it had ever been, that voice. It reverberated inside her skull.

And it was *right*. What else could she do? What else?

IN! IN! IN! IN!

Cassie's answer was less than a whisper.

'Yes . . .'

It was as if her whole body was slammed by a gigantic force that didn't stop when it hit her but went straight through her skin, straight through bone and flesh. She heard Estelle's scream of triumph. Then silence – deafening silence.

The spirit was inside her.

Cassie was sealed in a bubble. For what felt like long, long moments, there was only peace and awe. She felt the muscles of her face move, change. Her features twisted, exaggerated. But she felt no fear.

This is it, then?

This is it. I like it . . .

This power?

Yes . . .

Dreamlike, in slow motion, Cassie reached into her jacket and closed her hand around the knife. It was alive: just like her. Beneath her fingers the creatures squirmed, ecstatic. Power poured out of them, swirled in her blood, streamed back into the knife and out again in a vibrant, electric circuit. She didn't laugh, had no urge to gloat – just to fight. She felt her muscles tense as Brigitte and Katerina flung themselves towards her, but she hardly registered their bloodcurdling cries of attack. Everything seemed to be moving at half-speed. Cassie was filled with power, drowning in it. Her and the spirit. All power, all *one*.

She sprang into the air, leaping effortlessly at her adversaries, and her body was more a force of nature than a human being. Her fist was lightning, slashing at Katerina, sending her somersaulting backwards. Her other hand a thunderclap, snapping towards Brigitte's chest, and the woman staggered away, staring mesmerised at the knife in Cassie's clenched fingers.

Lightly she leaped at Brigitte again. The knife was alive, the creatures on the hilt singing for her. There was a pattern to their squirming movements, she realised: it all made sense. It was a dance. The creatures were in harmony. Marvelling at their elegant movements, she slashed at the blonde monster.

But this time, Brigitte was ready. She dodged Cassie's blow and whipped around her, quick as a flash, her fist connecting a hammering blow against the back of Cassie's skull. Cassie lurched forward, shaking her head vigorously as her vision blurred with the impact.

'Did you think it would be that easy, scholarship?' Katerina spat, springing in at her. 'Hah!'

Cassie blocked the demon girl's foot before it connected with her chin. Grabbing Katerina's leg, she launched her metres into the air with a tremendous roar.

Before she could press home the attack, though, Brigitte was on her back, her arms locked around Cassie's neck, choking her.

Cassie flung herself back on to the ground, and heard the wind burst out of Brigitte's lungs. Her arms went limp, and Cassie leaped up and flipped over, smashed her fist into Brigitte's face and dug the knife deep into her shoulder. Brigitte howled in agony.

'Mother!' screamed Katerina.

Springing up to face the daughter's attack, Cassie struck out with knife, and slammed the hilt against Katerina's head. Squealing with pain, the girl thudded, semi-conscious, on to the muddy ground. Lightning flared across the clouds again, and thunder reverberated, as Cassie crouched over Katerina's prone form and raised the blade high.

Her eyes burned and everything was red again. She liked it. She *loved* it.

Cassie's head was buzzing, her thoughts were a jumble of rage.

'I should end you, you bitch. You tried to kill us. Tried to kill us all!'

Us?

Jake and Isabella. And me and . . .

Cassie blinked hard, trying to still the fizzing anger so

she could think straight. Who else had Katerina tried to harm? She breathed deeply and turned her face skywards. Freezing rain stung her skin, reminding her she was vulnerable. Mortal.

Human . . .

'Estelle!' she gasped.

Oh, God. All of Estelle was still inside her. Right inside her body and mind. Cassie could feel her there. Uniting. Becoming one with her. Completing the task that the joining ritual had begun. Soon she would be a part of Cassie for ever. Unless . . .

Shutting her eyes, she focused all her will. Not superhuman power, Cassie thought, just the strength of her own mind. Her own soul. She began to feel a change, something moving, shifting. As she struggled, pushing against the force within, a familiar voice returned once more.

Cassandra? Stop! What are you doing?

'This isn't right,' Cassie said. 'I can't let this happen, Estelle! I shouldn't have let—'

NO!

Keeping her eyes squeezed shut, Cassie gritted her teeth as she felt her skin begin to shimmer, hot with the energy she was trying to force out.

Cassandra! Stop! Don't do this to me! I want to be whole!

'I'm sorry,' Cassie cried. 'I'm so sorry!'

Her head spun, and suddenly the heat across her skin dissipated. She'd done it. The power was close, but divided once more. Cassie panted, finally opening her eyes as cold rain mingled with her warm tears.

And from somewhere inside there came a wailing cry of pain and grief.

CHAPTER TWENTY-SEVEN

Once again, Cassie's energy was drained. Suddenly she was trembling, scared and alone, in the darkness. Instinctively, her hands flew up to feel her face. It was back to normal.

She staggered away from the prostrate forms of Katerina and Brigitte. In front of her, the Swedish Cottage loomed like a threatening behemoth, its flags flapping wildly, and now she was frightened again.

Don't be afraid! Let me back in, and there'll be no question of fear!

'Estelle?' she whispered in a trembling voice. 'I can't let that happen again.'

But Cassandra, my dear, now you've felt the possibilities . . .

'No. Estelle, I'm sorry, I can't—'

Fine, my dear. No apologies. But now you know. You know

how it should be! You will *let me in eventually, Cassandra. Forever.*

Behind Cassie, someone swore softly. She spun on her heel to see Jake kneeling over Isabella, rubbing her hands and kissing her cold lips like some kind of supremely dishevelled Prince Charming.

'Jake? Is she OK!' She stumbled to his side.

'Leave her!' His yelp was angry and scared. 'She's coming round.'

'OK,' she mumbled. She stared at the knife in her hand, now inert and inanimate. Blood glistened on the blade. A wave of nausea swept through her and the weapon toppled from her fingers to the ground.

At a sound, she turned. Brigitte was dragging her daughter to her feet, both of them eyeing Cassie with terror. They looked so ridiculously ordinary now – bleeding, smeared with mud, and soaked to their pale skin – Cassie couldn't even summon the energy to be angry. She watched, empty of all feeling, as the pair stumbled away into the shadows of Central Park. But something drew her closer to the dense trees where they'd vanished.

The pit of the Living Soil was entirely gone now. The ground was healed, the sodden turf showing not so much as a mark.

'Jake,' she whispered, closing her eyes. 'Let's get out of here.'

Between them, Jake and Cassie half-carried the groggy Isabella from the park, Jake insisting that the west side was closer. He seemed desperate to be out of Central Park and he was beginning to shake violently by the time they made it on to the streets. Delayed shock, thought Cassie.

Finally, they left the rainswept park behind and swung blindly into a narrow alley. Jake took a ragged breath. 'What the hell happened back there?' he snapped. His face was drained and there were dark bruises under his eyes, but his voice was full of accusation.

'I stopped you getting buried alive, that's what happened.' Cassie barely had the energy to raise her voice above a whisper.

He stared at her, his face a picture of disgust. 'What *are* you, Cassie?'

What was she? Didn't know, didn't care. There was a lead weight on her brain and an even heavier one in her gut. What had she done?

'You *killed* Vaughan. That FBI guy? And then . . .' He trailed off.

'I didn't mean to.'

'But you did, Cassie. You did.'

'Jake, not now. I can't think.' Stepping back from them both, Cassie rubbed her face hard with the palms of her hands, her breathing shallow and rapid. Suddenly she didn't want to look at him. Was there still a trace of red in her eyes?

'Jake, leave her alone.' Isabella's voice surprised them both, and they turned. She looked exhausted, but her speech was clear. 'What about you? What did Vaughan and Brigitte do, did they hurt you?'

'No. Not really. They came for me when I was asleep. Before I knew what was happening, they'd taken me to the park.' Once more he took a pace towards Cassie. 'Did you know what would happen? What they were planning? Why did you have the knife? You took it from my room, didn't you? Did you know what they were going to do with us, Cassie? Is that something you freaks all know about, you sick—' He broke off, shaking with what seemed to Cassie like a mixture of fear and disgust.

Had she known? Had she known what she would end up doing?

Maybe . . .

Maybe she'd *wanted* it.

Otherwise, why had she been so hell-bent on finding the knife, on doing everything just as Estelle ordered? Twisting her fingers into her hair, Cassie gave a low groan that came out as a growl. Her head still felt like a lump of stone yet it didn't seem to belong to her at all. Jake's hectoring voice was a long, long way away. Nothing mattered except the vortex of emptiness that was growing inside her, spinning into a greater and greater void.

'I need to feed,' she whispered as her legs gave way beneath her.

She couldn't focus. Vaguely, she knew she was being dragged further into the alley, propped against a brick wall between a fire escape and some restaurant bins. A gentle hand tipped her head back and stroked her face.

'She's in a bad way, Jake.' Isabella's voice sounded as if it came from the bottom of a deep well.

'So what? Isabella, leave her. Let's go.'

'No, Jake. No.'

A silence, during which Cassie heard her own breathing, rapid and shallow and hungry. Her fingers twitched, seeking to grab Isabella but only scraping uselessly on cobbles.

'Wait, what are you going to . . . ? No! No *way*, Isabella!'

'I've told you before, Jake.' Isabella's tone was determined. 'Stay out of this. It's got nothing to do with you.'

Hear, hear, thought Cassie woozily. Stay out of it, Jake . . .

'Absolutely not. I won't let you!'

'You can't stop me. Take your hands off me!'

To Cassie, the face-off seemed to last forever. Her own body seemed impossibly distant from her, yet the core of hunger was intolerable. She was just beginning to wish, despite herself, she'd left Jake to his shallow, unthinkable grave . . .

'OK, OK. Sorry. Come on, Isabella, please!'

'Jake, no! We'd be dead if it wasn't for Cassie!'

'*You* could be dead *because* of her!'

'You think?' Isabella's voice was tense. 'Let me tell you, Jake Johnson: none of this is Cassie's fault. She is what she is, but she is also our friend. She would give her *life* for us! She almost *did*! Fair is fair. I'm willing to risk mine for her.'

'Isabella, you think I can stand that? I love you! I *love* you. Don't do this.'

There was a pause.

'Jake . . . I love you too. But if you won't stay here and help me – help *us* – you can go to hell.' Her words were tough, but Isabella's voice was trembling with emotion.

Jake stared at them both, disbelieving, love and loathing warring in his eyes. He took a step forward, and for a moment Cassie thought Isabella's words had done enough to persuade him. Then his mouth hardened, and he turned his back and walked away. A moment later, he had vanished into the night.

Isabella silently watched him go. Then she knelt in front of Cassie, loosening her coat collar, cupping her face in her cold hands and moving to put her lips to her friend's.

No, no, not like that, it's too dangerous . . .

But Cassie couldn't help herself. Her fingers flailed in Isabella's glossy hair. Feebly, she held her head up and whimpered.

The surge of energy slammed into her like a high-voltage current. Isabella's mouth was pressed against her own, and Cassie leaned forward, drawing hungrily. The energy was incredible, irresistible, but that spinning vortex of hunger inside was sucking it into her with no hesitation. Isabella's skin paled to whiteness.

But Cassie was determined this time. She absolutely would not lose control. The sacrifice Isabella had just made meant she would not allow it. After a moment, she forced herself to stop. It was over. She was so, so glad when it was over.

'Jake . . .' Cassie said hoarsely.

'I know. It's OK.' Isabella's voice was bleak.

Ashamed, Cassie clambered to her feet. But physically she felt stronger than ever. She scooped Isabella off the ground and held her tightly, tears stinging her eyelids. 'Thank you,' she choked.

Isabella squeezed her friend tightly by way of reply. When she spoke, her voice was racked with emotion. 'He'll come back. Won't he?'

Cassie took a deep breath. 'I don't know, Isabella,' she said honestly. 'I really don't know.'

CHAPTER TWENTY-EIGHT

'The Council of the Elders is called to order. Sir Alric Darke presiding.'

The atmosphere in the Trustees' Room couldn't have been more different from the last time she'd sat here, nervous and alone. This time Cassie stood, relaxed but determined. She felt comfortable in the room's grand elegance, and she wasn't overawed by the row of Elders seated behind the long table. They seemed smaller now.

Studying the line of faces, she met each gaze individually. Some of the figures, even the most familiar ones, were fidgeting uncertainly. Such a meeting was unprecedented, Sir Alric had told her. This ought to be interesting . . .

'You can't call the meeting to order until Brigitte and Vaughan get here,' objected the female senator, tapping a sleek fountain pen on her leather organiser.

'Brigitte Svensson and Andrew Vaughan will not be attending this Council.' Sir Alric ignored the collective intake of breath that greeted this announcement. 'For reasons that will become clear, I think we may assume that they send their apologies.'

'Then let's hear it,' drawled an A-list Hollywood actor. 'What's this about?'

Cassie looked at him coldly, unintimidated by his famous devilish grin. 'I'm here to register my protest about your last decision.'

A red-haired supermodel exchanged glances with her neighbour. 'That would be the decision regarding the Johnson boy?'

'That would be the decision regarding *Jake*, yes.'

'May I ask,' murmured the actor, 'what business it might be of yours? Or in fact, how you even came to know about it?'

Cassie breathed steadily, ignoring his last question. She was determined not to lose control and scratch his eyes out.

'First, he's my . . .' A faint pause. 'He's my friend. Second, he's an innocent party. And third, what you did was wrong.'

While her words sank in, there were a few muttered exchanges and even a gruff laugh or two. The senator

272

smirked and sat back in her chair.

'I hardly think that a recently converted, half-Few mongrel can appreciate the very complex issues involved in this case. Sir Alric, I suggest that your convening of this Council was extraordinarily ill-judged. The meeting should be terminated at once. We're all busy people.'

Mongrel? The insolence!

Cassie felt her spine stiffen with shared indignation, but still she almost laughed at Estelle's mortified tone. Time for the gloves to come off.

'Actually, the issues aren't complex at all. I think that even a politician should be capable of understanding what I have to say.'

'I beg your pardon?' The senator went crimson.

The supermodel sniggered, and so did Estelle.

That's telling them, my dear.

'How many of you,' asked Cassie, 'have checked on Jake Johnson in the Confine?'

'Checking isn't necessary, my dear,' a cardinal told her with a little smile. 'He's perfectly safe there. The Confine isn't an unpleasant place. Not by any means.'

'So it's not much like the Living Soil, then?'

That shut them up. The cardinal went a colour to match his cassock.

'My dear Miss Bell,' he coughed. 'The very mention of

that is a blasphemy. Use of the Living Soil was banned centuries ago. Let us not hear any more of it.'

'Oh, up until last night, it was still very much in use,' said Cassie calmly, 'and you almost condemned Jake Johnson to it.'

The uproar was satisfying.

'How *dare* you—'

'Darke, this is unacceptable.'

'I demand an explanation!'

'Then Cassandra,' murmured Sir Alric quietly, 'will give you one.'

Cassie shot him a grateful look, but her expression hardened as she studied the row of Elders.

'Brigitte and Vaughan have made fools of the lot of you,' she said coldly. 'They've been taking prisoners from the Confine and feeding them to the Living Soil for years. I can show you the place where it happened. You can determine how true it is for yourselves. If you can face it.'

'Indeed?' drawled the actor. 'And you can prove this?'

'If you don't believe me,' retorted Cassie, pointing, 'ask him.'

All eyes in the room swivelled from Cassie to the handsome features of Sir Alric. He cleared his throat.

'Cassie came to me with her story last night. Needless to say I was as shocked as the rest of you, but I did visit the place she described. I am afraid what she has told you is true – there are human corpses under the ground there. I have also been to the Confine.' He paused. 'It was empty. I fear there can be little doubt that all those who were being held there have been fed to the Living Soil, here in New York.'

No one moved; no one spoke. The supermodel had paled, and even the senator had her eyes shut and her hand over her mouth.

'My God . . .' whispered the old cardinal.

Sir Alric gazed steadily at Cassie. 'Cassandra, I can assure you that none of the other Elders were aware of the abomination you witnessed. I hope you believe that.'

'I'm trying to.' Cassie clasped her hands tightly behind her back, digging her nails into her palms. 'But even if that's true, even if you didn't know about the Living Soil, you are all still responsible. You voted to send Jake to the Confine, along with God knows how many other people whose only crime was to know too much about the Few. But you never bothered to *check* on them, did you? You didn't want to know – out of sight, out of mind. So Vaughan and Brigitte were able to do whatever they wanted with them.'

Nineteen pairs of eyes were focused on her. She clenched her hands tighter so they wouldn't shake.

'And what's more – your *Confine*? It's a jail. I don't care how fancy it is, it's a prison for innocents, and that's wrong. You want to protect the secret of the Few? Well, here's the deal – you work out another way to do it. I want the Confine closed. Now. And if I ever hear of anybody else vanishing, if anything happens to Jake Johnson, or any other innocent person, I'll be the fat lady in the Few's last act. You hear me? I'll be singing at the top of my voice. I'll go to the cops. I'll go to the FBI. I'll go to CNN and Fox News and the *New York Times* and the *Washington Post* and, damn it, I'll go to the *National Enquirer*.'

Breathless with fury, she forced her voice to calm. There was redness in her eyes. Just enough: she mustn't let it go too far . . . The power bubbled like a physical thing, just under her skin, but now *she* was controlling *it*, rather than vice versa.

'I don't care how influential you are, there are still plenty of influential people who *aren't* Few. I'll go to them, I'll tell them everything. I'll tell all the *normal* people. Because there still are some, you know? Normal, decent individuals who don't have to steal their life-force from other people.'

'And you,' the Hollywood actor reminded her silkily, 'are not one of them.'

'No,' she spat. 'But I remember what it was like. I remember who I was. Comes of being a mongrel, I guess.'

'If we go down, you will suffer with us, Miss Bell.' The senator's voice was frigid.

'Maybe so, senator. But I'll do it anyway. And I know what you're thinking: that you could just put *me* in your precious Confine. Lock me away. Well . . .' Cassie forced a grin, summoning all her chutzpah. And that wasn't so hard when she could already see that at least half of them were visibly afraid of her. '. . . You can put me in the Confine, *but can you keep me there?*'

Calmly reaching out with a tentacle of force, Cassie gently lifted the fountain pen from the senator's numb fingers and snapped it neatly in two.

The senator let out a choking gasp. The rest of the Elders seemed dumbstruck.

How's that for control, Sir Alric?

And was she mistaken, or was there just a hint of pride in his granite eyes?

Sir Alric Darke rapped the silver gavel, very gently, so that it made the sweetest of ringing sounds.

'So, ladies and gentlemen, shall we put it to a vote?'

CHAPTER TWENTY-NINE

Cassie lifted her phone as it vibrated silently in her hand. Yet again she studied the glowing display.

1 New Message
from
Patrick Malone

Once more her thumb moved to the keypad. Once more it gently pressed *Delete*.

She rolled over in bed and peered over at Isabella's shape in the darkness. It had taken hours for her to finally fall asleep. Cassie wasn't so lucky. Whenever she closed her eyes she saw what would have happened if she hadn't stopped Katerina and Brigitte in time. If she hadn't taken the knife. If she hadn't listened to Estelle . . .

Estelle had been there when she needed her. When it

came to the crunch, it was Estelle that she turned to. So what did that mean for Cassie? *Was* she a monster, just like the people from whom she had been trying to protect her friends? She wasn't even sure she could call Jake her friend now – it seemed clear he wouldn't welcome it, at least. Since he'd left them in the alleyway, there had been no sign of him. He'd vanished just as surely as the Few knife. Cassie had searched all over the grounds of the Swedish Cottage when she'd returned there with Sir Alric, but the blade had vanished. Of course, any passer-by could have picked it up, but somehow Cassie knew that Jake had it.

Why had he gone back for it, that reminder of everything he hated? To try to kill Katerina? Or was he thinking he might need to use it against Cassie herself, some time in the future?

The future . . . Cassie sighed. Who knew what that held?

I do. I know . . .

Ever since Cassie had allowed her fully into her mind and body, there had been a new calmness to Estelle's voice. As though she was certain that Cassie would eventually let her in again, permanently.

'It's never going to happen, Estelle.'

Cassie was adamant. But what did it mean, to give that

279

up? What was she losing? The incredible feeling of power that the joining had given her still resonated in Cassie's mind, like the memory of a drug. It felt like a struggle every moment just to keep the desire at bay. But struggle she would. She couldn't risk hurting Isabella, losing control, doing any more damage. She didn't like what she'd become – what she had the potential to become . . .

Sooner or later, you'll have to embrace it, my dear!

Cassie jumped as she heard a soft knock at the door. Jake? She almost leaped for the door, glancing at her blotched face in the wardrobe mirror. At least her eyes were back to a respectable yellow-green.

Opening the door, she had to steady herself as she saw who stood there.

'Ranjit.'

She had to keep her breathing even, however hard it was. Something twisted in her chest, but she beat back the longing, and kept her distance.

'Cassie. Hi.' The handsome Indian boy clenched and unclenched his fists. She'd never seen him look so nervous and unhappy. It didn't mean she was letting him off the hook, though. Mindful of Isabella, she slipped out into the corridor and pulled the door to behind her.

'I'm surprised to see you here.'

He took a wounded breath. 'Cassie – I'm sorry. About everything.'

'You heard the story, then?'

'I've spoken to Sir Alric.' He looked at his hands. 'And he's spoken to me.'

'Back to normal, then. I'm getting talked about behind my back. My ears'll be as red as my eyes.'

'You don't think I wanted – needed – to know what happened?' His eyes flashed, and just for an instant their amber became tinged with scarlet. Scrutinising him, Cassie nodded thoughtfully to herself. Swallowing, Ranjit took a step back.

'I'm sure you wanted to know, Ranjit. Course, you'd have seen it all first-hand if you'd been around to help us.' She swallowed. Even now, despite everything, the last thing she wanted to do was hurt him. But he needed hurting – she'd had her share from him. It was his turn.

'I'm sorry.' His face was very solemn. 'But that doesn't mean I could have done things any other way.'

'Everybody gets a choice, Ranjit. Everybody's got free will. We are human, after all.'

He gave her a sad smile. 'That's a matter of opinion.'

Cassie folded her arms, stared over his shoulder. 'Why are you here?'

'To ask you . . . to be careful. Please, Cassie. I don't

want anything to happen to you.'

'Bit late for that.' She shook her head bitterly.

'I'm talking about the Council. The Elders. You don't know what they're capable of, Cassie.'

'Now, where have I heard that before?' She put a finger to her chin. 'Oh, yes. That's what *they* said about *me*.'

'I'm serious. They've had to accept your demands this time – they couldn't deny that what Brigitte and Vaughan were doing was wrong – but the Elders don't like to be crossed, Cassie. Please be careful. For your own sake.' He took a breath. 'And mine.'

'I see. It's a self-preservation thing.'

With a sigh, Ranjit slid down the wall to the floor, resting his arms on his knees. After a moment's hesitation, Cassie sat down at his side.

'Ranjit.' She picked at a hangnail, her voice quiet. 'Why are you here? Really?'

She knew the answer she wanted – for him to tell her he'd been wrong, that he never should have abandoned her. That he loved her. She needed him to say that.

Ranjit turned his head so he was looking into her eyes. That brought his face, his lips, so very close. She could smell him. His skin, his hair, his essence. Cassie struggled to control her breathing. In, out. In, out. No panting, now. She felt dangerously vulnerable under his gaze.

'Really?' he said. 'Truly? Because I wanted – I *needed* to see you. I've missed you like hell. I wish to God that I didn't have to do what I did. You have to believe me, Cassie. But I still had to do it. And I just wanted to explain myself, so that maybe, just maybe, you won't hate me so much.' He hesitated, his eyes imploring.

Cassie nodded. 'Go on.'

He turned his head away to stare at the floor again. 'And I need to tell you why we can't be together any more.'

Those words hurt so much, and so unexpectedly, she had to pause for long moments.

'Right.'

He took a deep breath. 'I wanted to be with you at the Council. The night of the meeting, I was ready. In my room. About to come to get you. And . . .'

She sighed. Why did he expect her to make it easier for him? 'And?'

'And Sir Alric came to see me.'

'I see. So you left me alone because you had a more important meeting.'

'You don't understand!' he snapped. 'He told me what he was expecting that night – at the Council. He told me he'd have to fight tooth and nail just to keep you out of the Confine.'

'Did he really?' Cassie arched an eyebrow. 'It didn't show.'

'I think it's true. He said he had to convince the Elders he could control you. That he could monitor you within the Academy, restrain you, *train* you. And . . .' Ranjit took a breath. 'And that he couldn't do that if I was there with you.'

Cassie bit a nail. 'What? Why?'

'Because we shouldn't be together, Cassie.'

When she could finally breathe out, the sigh was shaky. 'I see. Well, in that case there's more nothing to explain. *Sir Alric* has spoken, so—'

'Cassie, it's not like that. Please listen. There's . . . there's so much to explain. It's not that I don't – it's not that I don't like you. Very . . . very much. It's not that I don't desperately want to be with you.'

Cassie let out a short, mirthless laugh. 'Hard to see what it is, then.'

Miserably, he raked his hands through his hair. 'It's our *spirits*, Cassie. You must feel it too. The way things are between us? So volatile? One second wanting to tear each other's hair out, the next wanting to tear each other's clothes off? And what happened last time we were together. Remember? You think *you* have trouble controlling yourself? Well, so do I. Especially around you.'

She bit her lip, watched his tormented profile.

'Yeah.' She hesitated.

'Cassie, Sir Alric had already explained it to me that night he called me back into his office after he saw us together. I didn't want to believe him. I tried to ignore it. I argued. But what he told me is right. If you think about it, you'll know it's true. We bring out the worst in each other, Cassandra.' He shook his head sadly.

'Yes we do, Ranjit.' She got to her feet, suddenly desperate not to cry in front of him. Not to grab him, hang on to him, beg him not to go.

She had trouble controlling herself . . .

'Not us, I mean what's inside us. Our spirits bring out the worst in each other, that's what Sir Alric told me. God, I'm doing this so badly . . .' He took an exasperated breath. 'We'll become worse, Cassie – we'll egg each other on. We're like a pair of evil twins. You know what else he said?'

'Surprise me.'

'If I had shown up at the Council meeting,' he said intently, 'he'd've let you go to the Confine.'

'He did what?'

'He said he wouldn't have a choice. If I'd insisted on supporting you he'd have cast his vote to imprison you. For your protection and everyone else's. So what choice did I have?'

She put her head in her hands. 'The choice to fight for me?'

'Oh, Cassie, don't you see?' He touched her hair, and it was like a tiny electric shock. 'I tried. But I couldn't ignore the basic fact that he was right.'

'You *so* do not have to explain any more.' She slapped his hand aside and stepped back, her voice shaking though she wished it wouldn't. 'I'll be fine on my own, Ranjit. I always have been. It was a big mistake, getting dependent again. Not like me at all.'

She stepped back deliberately from him. 'After all, regardless of our spirits, you'd never have been there for me. You weren't there when I really needed you, and now I know you never will be, because you're a bloody *coward*. You won't fight. You'll just take to your heels and *hide*!' She shook her head furiously. 'I fight, Ranjit. I'm not running. But if you want to, you go ahead. You run for your immortal life.'

Scrambling to his feet, he stared at her, but he couldn't move.

'Go on, Ranjit. Get out of here.' She reached back for the handle of her door, fumbled it open, clutching the cold metal to stop her hand shaking. 'And don't worry your pretty little head about me. It seems I'm the devil in disguise.'

Stepping back through the door, she watched his stunning, devastated face. She *made* herself watch it, to prove her immunity. She didn't take her eyes away from that beautiful gaze, not till she'd finally closed the door on it. Not till she could at last press her forehead to the wood and let the tears dribble down to the floor.

Only for a moment, though. She wasn't going to indulge the stupid tears. There was nothing to cry about. Nothing. She didn't need him. She could look after herself.

She could even ignore the tiny voice inside, begging her, pleading with her.

That can't be it. It can't be over. It can't be the end . . .

And then her own sad, plaintive inner voice was drowned out anyway.

I see. You're letting them go. We're letting them go. Well, perhaps we don't need them after all . . .

'Estelle?' she whispered. 'Are you sure?'

A comforting sensation of warmth trickled down her spine, spreading like an embrace. Her fingertips tingled; her eyes burned. Warmth, comfort, power . . .

Yes, Cassandra, my love, I'm sure now. We can do this. You are strong. Stronger than him. I chose you well. And I'll always be here for you! Always.

Yes, thought Cassie, I know that now.

And of course it isn't the end, my darling. We're only just getting started . . .

Turn the page to read an exclusive extract from the third book in the Darke Academy series: Divided Souls.

DIVIDED SOULS

This was no chore.

Yusuf Ahmed smiled down at the girl who sat on the velvet couch, far more in his hungry eyes than the prosaic lust of a boy for a girl. Touching her jaw with a finger, he drew a gentle line to her chin: tantalising himself and her, feeling the hunger grow and letting it.

'Another *raki*?' He proffered the carafe.

'I think I've had enough.' Her voice was teasing.

He gave a soft laugh. *Yes*, he thought. *Yes, I think you probably have.*

Yusuf took a small step away from her, enjoying the masochistic kick of prolonging the wait. He was hungry, but not so hungry he would rush it.

Raising his eyes to the open window and the balmy night, he let himself soak up the beauty of it: the moon on the Bosphorus; the lights of a cruise ship strung like a glittering diamond necklace. High and hazy in the warm evening, the dome and minarets of the Blue Mosque gleamed like chalcedony.

It reminded him vaguely of Sacre Coeur, of last autumn term in Paris, when everything had changed. When things had begun, for the first time in so very long, to go awry for the Few. When that scruffy waif of a scholarship girl, Cassie Bell, had turned up at the Academy and been shockingly chosen by Estelle Azzedine, then tricked into becoming the new host the old woman needed for her powerful spirit.

He wished now that he'd never got involved . . . though he still remembered with some relish the frisson of excitement at the joining ceremony, the sense of entitlement and arrogance and power. He vividly recalled the Bell girl's fury as they held her down at Estelle's mercy, and he recalled too the unexpected pity – and fear – he had felt in himself. Because it had gone wrong so fast. The joining ritual interrupted; part of Estelle's spirit joined with Cassie, part of it shut out in the void; and the Few left as stunned as if a bomb had gone off in their midst.

Yusuf shook his head. A new term had now begun, and the girl Cassie seemed to be settling into being one of the Few. He was actually glad. They were all glad. Or most of them were . . . So who knew what brighter turn things might take for the Few? Including himself.

Closing his eyes, he inhaled warm air scented with night flowers, sea breeze, petrol fumes and charcoal smoke. Gods, he was going to love it here in Istanbul. This was his final term at the Academy, and he felt a keen sense of regret mingled with the anticipation. His future glowed before him with wealth, success and influence: how could it be otherwise? But still, he'd miss the comradeship, the secrets, the power of being one of the Few at the Academy. It had been fun.

A light hand touched his arm. Yusuf turned to the girl, suddenly aching with the beauty of the night and with hungry longing.

She blinked. Her eyes were already a little unfocused and distant, her smile trembling on her lips as if she'd half-forgotten it was there.

Good . . .

He set down his own glass and took her face between his hands. She was lovely, with her golden heart-shaped face and her huge dark eyes. Her lips parted and she made a small sound: it might have been desire or bewilderment, but he no longer cared. She'd drunk what he'd offered her. She wouldn't remember.

For one moment longer, he hesitated. Feeding like this was forbidden, because it was too dangerous. But for that very reason the thrill made it irresistible. And Yusuf was nothing if not experienced. He was strong, he was skilled.

And *damn*, he was hungry.

Gripping her face, he brought her lips fiercely against his own. He felt the momentary simple pleasure of human contact. Then, inside his chest, the spirit pulsed and energy gushed into his veins. His eyes widened, reddening.

As the girl made a small moan of protest, he forced himself back under control. He wouldn't hurt her: that wasn't how he got his kicks. Relaxing his hold, he intensified the kiss, feeling life-energy thrill to his nerve-endings. Oh, this was feeding, this was satisfaction, this was *bliss*.

His senses sharpened, smell and taste suddenly acute. He could hear the thrum and beat of the city, the throb of the cruise ship's engines. He could hear a soft footstep. And then a whisper said his name.

Yusuf Ahmeeeed . . .

Had he misheard? Releasing the girl, he went still, listening intently.

He'd chosen his place well: this secluded room with its romantic arches and nooks, above the restaurant in Old Istanbul. He'd paid the owner *extremely* well because he'd made it perfectly clear he did *not* want to be disturbed.

How did they know his name? Was it someone who knew him from the Academy . . . ?

He shivered at the thought. That was trouble he didn't want, not right at the end of his school career. Unauthorised feeding, in a forbidden manner? It wasn't beyond possibility that he could be kicked out, like Katerina Svensson after the business with the Bell girl. Sir Alric took his rules very, very seriously . . .

Silent, every sense alert, he turned towards the darkness beyond the window arch. He stepped closer, then became preternaturally still as his eyes searched the night. Below him was a courtyard and the balcony extended round three sides of it, draped with shadows.

There. Against a cracked tile wall, one shadow darted past quickly.

Someone was spying on him. One who knew his name. Taunting *him*: a sixth former, one of the most powerful Few! The spirit inside him kindled, but this time with rage. How *dare* they!

He'd satisfied his hunger, and now the romantic moment was lost too: one more reason to turn his fury on the intruder. He touched the girl's face. Gradually, gently, she came back to herself, eyes focusing, mouth curving into a more determined smile.

'Aren't you going to kiss me, then?'

If only you knew, he thought dryly.

'Sorry, *habibi*. I've had a text, it's an emergency. You have to go.'

Her sulky pout was delicious to behold. He laughed. 'I'll see you tomorrow night. I'll make it up to you, yes?'

'Oh, yes. You certainly will.' She winked. Drawing a finger down his chest in farewell, she blew him a tantalising kiss and was gone.

Yusuf gave one last yearning sigh, but his muscles were already tensing for a chase. Light and swift, he vaulted through the arch and out on to the rickety balcony. The dark figure had had plenty of time to make an escape, but only when he dropped lightly down to the courtyard did Yusuf see it break into a run. *Foolish*, he thought.

The figure managed to keep several steps ahead of him as they chased through the alleys of Sultanahmet; its footsteps were almost as deft and light as Yusuf's own. It was growing dark and lonely as they travelled through the streets, the sounds of the city muffled by distance, as if he had pursued the shadow into another time zone. No one around.

Slowing, he realised with surprise that the figure was heading up the steps of an outbuilding beside the Hagia Sophia. Was it a mausoleum? Still, Yusuf felt no fear. He approached the entrance and realised the crypt was empty of people, closed for renovation. But as he entered, despite his expectations the place was not dark. Above him a domed Byzantine ceiling gleamed in the light of hundreds of candles.

Candles . . . ?

He stopped, ears pricked. Every inlaid door leading off the room was open.

Yusuf was very alert now. Beyond the vast atrium, the place was a maze of arches and passageways, and whoever the prowler was, he was hiding. And he was very good at it . . .

Yusuf felt himself thrill at this stealthy hunt. Not a wasted evening, really. An opponent was almost as much of a kick as a lover. He was going to teach this upstart a lesson.

Ha! Movement, sharp, at the corner of his eye. *There*, beyond that arch with its chipped and faded gilding. Yusuf moved, swift and silent as a cat.

The anteroom was small, with fretwork cloisters and half-destroyed blue mosaics, and the glow of candlelight didn't penetrate the shadows beyond the pillars. There was no exit: it was a trap. Yusuf halted, smiling wryly. Time to turn the tables and flush him out, this insolent stalker.

'Show yourself.' His voice, clear and commanding,

echoed through archways.

In response there was only silence. He turned a slow half-circle, eyeing every corner, every shadow.

'There's nowhere to go. Face it.'

Still nothing. The flickering golden air was heavy with the stillness.

'Who the hell are you? Show yourself *now*.'

A movement, a sound behind him. It might only have been a footfall, but it was close. Too close.

Yusuf spun on his heel, tensed to strike, furious at the audacity. The glint of a smile met him, and then another, more sinister glint.

'*You?* What the hell—'

Yusuf staggered back, flinging up his hands in horror. He didn't even have time to scream. Couldn't run. Couldn't shut his terrified eyes. He only felt, for the first and last time, a crushing and paralysing terror as the figure lunged at him.

Then every candle in the building went out, and Yusuf's world turned to absolute blackness.